"I want to take you home," Jay whispered

"Oh." Amanda shivered, though she wasn't chilly.

"I want you in my bed." He cupped her cheeks with his broad hands and kissed her gently on the lips. "Naked."

"Uh-huh." Wouldn't it be something to have him lying next to her? Amanda thought. Kissing her all over? Stroking her thigh, her back? *Fulfilling all her sexual fantasies.*

"Is that a yes?"

The tip of her tongue glided across his upper lip. She moaned as she deepened the kiss, and he felt her nipples pebbling against his shirt.

"Let's go get a cab." Jay's mind raced. He'd give her a long leisurely bath, soaping her from head to toe, with special attention to the important parts in between.

Amanda was so much more than he'd imagined. He should have guessed that when he read her fantasies online. He was going to make every fantasy come true. *Starting now...in his bed.*

Dear Reader,

Have you ever wished that some special guy would see the real you, the you inside, the you who doesn't have bad hair days, wear old-lady underwear or spill red wine on your boss's white carpet? And because this man sees how incredible you are, he can't live without you?

I've wished for just that, many times. I've longed for Mr. Right to pick me out of the crowd, then sweep me off my feet. While it hasn't happened to me...yet, I know it can happen. I've seen it happen.

Writing about Amelia and Jay filled me with hope and promise. They had to get through a lot before they found the brass ring (diamond ring?), but neither of them gave up. I came to care a great deal about these two, and I hope you do, too.

Here's wishing you love and peace,

Jo Leigh

Books by Jo Leigh

HARLEQUIN BLAZE
2—GOING FOR IT
23—SCENT OF A WOMAN

HARLEQUIN TEMPTATION
727—TANGLED SHEETS
756—HOT AND BOTHERED
809—MS. TAKEN

SENSUAL SECRETS

Jo Leigh

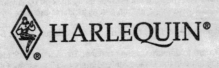

HARLEQUIN®

TORONTO • NEW YORK • LONDON
AMSTERDAM • PARIS • SYDNEY • HAMBURG
STOCKHOLM • ATHENS • TOKYO • MILAN • MADRID
PRAGUE • WARSAW • BUDAPEST • AUCKLAND

To my friends at Army Street—
thank you for your incredible support.
And of course, to Debbi. Without you, this wouldn't be!!!

ISBN 0-373-79038-4

SENSUAL SECRETS

Copyright © 2002 by Jolie Kramer.

Visit us at www.eHarlequin.com

Printed in U.S.A.

1

SOMETHING SHIFTED IN THE AIR. It wasn't a scent; the front door to the cyber café hadn't been opened. In fact, no breeze stirred. But she felt it, all right. Electrical. Sharp. The moment before lightning strikes. *Yes.*

Amelia Edwards's gaze moved surreptitiously to her right. David, who was in her poli-sci class at NYU, felt it, too. His shoulders, usually slumped forward in a perpetual hunch, had straightened. He ran a nervous hand through unruly dark hair.

She looked past David to a girl she'd seen several times before. Another student, if her backpack was any indication. Blond. Really pretty. Nibbling on her lower lip, thrusting out her chest, gaze darting to the door.

Everyone felt it. Not just Amelia. There was no law of physics to explain it. It was an X-file, a phenomenon, a mystery wrapped in an enigma. But she knew what it meant.

He was coming.

His name was Jay Wagner, and he owned the Harley shop next door. Slightly older than her—maybe twenty-six or -seven. Tall, with dark wavy hair that was a bit too long, and the most intense brown eyes she'd ever seen. When he walked into the room, everything else faded to shadow. Time slowed....

The wicked thoughts began.

Amelia's hand went to her hair—the top, the sides—checking for who knows what. A quick swipe of her lips with the tip of her tongue, a tug on her skirt.

Brian, the owner of the café, started a CD. Stevie Ray Vaughn.

Her gaze flew to the door seconds before it opened.

He had on his leather jacket. Black. Black jeans, white T-shirt, black boots. Shades that hid his eyes completely. That made her think of secrets.

She guessed him to be around six-two. Lean, wiry, but strong. His hands fascinated her, with their elegant fingers and flexing tendons.

He let the door close behind him, then headed for the bar. Glasses still on, looking neither right nor left. But that was only the first part of the game. The real action would begin when he got to her table. He didn't have to pass this way. Her workstation was in the corner, hidden from prying eyes. But he made it a point to cross the room whenever she was there.

Sure enough, when he stood about five feet away, he took off his glasses. Tucked them in his pocket. Then his head turned toward her. She tried not to look at him, but she knew it was a useless struggle. He wouldn't leave until she met his gaze. Why? Why did he do this to her? He had to see that it embarrassed the dickens out of her. She felt herself turn three shades of scarlet. Did he enjoy the power? The way she squirmed?

And why, oh why, did she keep coming back here, day after day? And please, would someone explain why her heart sank if he didn't show up?

Another brief stab at resistance, then she gave it up. She focused on his chest first. His jacket. Then her gaze climbed slowly to his neck, the squared jaw.

She exhaled a breath she hadn't remembered holding. Then she stopped breathing altogether when her gaze moved those last few inches.

He locked on to her the moment she was in range. Like a heat-seeking missile, he wouldn't let her go now until he'd had his fun. His right brow arched with wry amusement, as if she were quaint, as if she were a child. His lips curved into the tiniest of smiles. But it was the challenge in his eyes that made her insides turn to mush.

They'd never spoken. She never had the nerve. But for weeks now, he'd played this game with her. Daring her. Inviting her.

A part of her wanted to meet the challenge. To walk up to him and kiss him, right here in the middle of the café with the music blaring and the rich scent of strong coffee in the air. Boy, that would wipe that smug smile away. It would be so great.

Unfortunately, she was a chicken. A big, fat, yellow chicken. Her cheeks burned hotter, and she forced her gaze back to her monitor. He'd won. Again. She sighed when he chuckled. Just like he had yesterday, and the day before.

She focused on the screen. The words she'd written moments ago seemed unfamiliar and disconnected. A paper due in four days. She saved the file to disk, then, with shaky fingers, typed the Web address for TrueConfessions.com. The familiar page filled the monitor screen as she logged in, using her screen name. *Good Girl.*

She winced at her propensity to tell it like it was, even when the truth was as boring as a cable-knit sweater. She was, indeed, a good girl. At twenty-four and a graduate student at NYU, she was an anomaly. A throwback to the days when girls got pinned and went steady. Only, she had no one in her life with whom to do either of those things, not to mention anything racier.

At the thought, she raised her head, only to see Jay still standing right in front of her. Closer now. Her face heated instantly as she realized her mistake. He'd always wandered off when she'd hidden behind work. But this time he'd stayed to stare, his gaze so intense that she wriggled in her seat.

He took a step toward her, and her heart reacted by pounding in her chest. When he took another, she forgot how to breathe. *Oh God.* He kept on coming, his boots clicking softly on the hardwood floor.

He reached the side of the table. Everything in her told her to run, to hide, at the very least to duck. But she sat perfectly still, her head back as she looked up at the most beautiful man she'd ever seen.

He smiled. Not a big grin. A slight upward curve of his lips. Then his hand lifted and she nearly died.

He was going to touch her. Pet her cheek. Only, his hand stopped inches away, then withdrew. She burned with embarrassment at his retreat, sure she would burst into flames any second.

His low chuckle made things infinitely worse. Perhaps sensing that she was going to pass out, his gaze shifted to her computer screen. She took advantage of the situation and gasped in a lungful of air.

"Good Girl," he whispered.

Her mouth opened. Nothing came out.

He chuckled again, the sound deep and sexy. Mercifully, he walked past her, heading toward his buddy Brian at the coffee bar.

She closed her eyes as she struggled to get her pulse to slow and her breath to normalize. He'd spoken to her. Directly. *Oh God.*

Despite the fact that he'd looked at her before, made her blush, she'd always felt invisible. She was, most of the time. In class. Around her gorgeous roommates. At the student lounge. People bumped into her all the time. They just didn't notice her, that's all.

But he'd spoken to her.

Her gaze darted to the girl across the way. Just as Amelia figured, the girl seemed upset. Jealous. Of *her.* Not that she wanted the blonde to feel bad...

Okay, so she did.

Amelia turned back to her computer. She'd paid for two hours, and she only had fifteen minutes left. Typing furiously, she tried to capture it all. The moment, the excitement, his whisper, the scent of leather.

It poured out of her, and she didn't even go back to correct the misspelled words.

But at the end, when it was all out there, her bubble burst. He might have noticed her. How could he help it? She was here all the time. And she blushed so hard she could stop traffic. He'd just been messing with her, that's all. Teasing. Which was such a shame. Such a heartbreak. Her aunt Grace used to tell her that no one ever died from being shy, but Amelia wasn't sure. People did die of loneliness. Of yearning.

The truth of the matter was that the Amelia she was on the inside was nothing like the person she was on the outside. She dressed more conservatively than was fashionable; her skirts were longer, her blouses looser. She wore her hair pulled back, most of the time in a bun, and her hair was her biggest vanity.

She'd grown used to being invisible. It was easier that way. No one expected anything much. Only…

She paused. Sighed. *The woman I am inside isn't shy. She's brazen and erotic and she dresses in sexy clothes and she feels beautiful,* she typed.

Amelia closed her eyes, letting her fingers work on the keyboard she knew so well.

If only someone could see how I ache for a touch. How I yearn to be set on fire by a kiss. If only he knew how I dreamed of him. How I longed for him to take me to the heights of ecstasy. Oh, who am I kidding? I want him to make love to me until we both die of starvation. I want him to do anything, everything. I want to go crazy, and stay crazy, with him.

The buzzer on her computer went off, and she didn't have the time or cash to extend her stay. She saved her journal, then she logged off the confession Web site. Moving as quietly and efficiently as she could, she collected her belongings, stood up and hurried outside, never once looking behind her to see if Jay noticed—but blushing all the same.

JAY WAITED while Brian poured a cup of coffee for a customer—another student. The place wasn't large or fancy, and it didn't have the Starbucks chairs or upscale coffee paraphernalia. But it did have six workstations, all linked to the Internet by high-speed, high-bandwidth T1 connections, which meant instant and immediate access to research material. And porn.

The decor owed more to sixties rock than good taste. Posters of Hendrix, Janis Joplin, The Grateful Dead were tacked on the odd wall, and *Rolling Stone* magazine was always available. Brian, who must have been a hippie in his past life, played current top-twenty songs, but only because he had to. Curious, Jay thought, that Brian had opened such a high-tech business. But Jay had to give it to him. Brian had made the café a success. At thirty-two, Brian made a mean pot of coffee, and he could hack into almost any computer system around. He made sure his customers were happy. It was a lesson Jay had taken to heart when he'd opened his Harley shop next door.

Brian finished up with his customer, and Jay gave him a nod. Brian came over with a pot of coffee in hand. "You need more java?"

"What's TrueConfessions.com?"

Brian shrugged. It was an unconscious habit, one that most people assumed meant he didn't know whatever was being asked of him. Jay knew better. The shrug was Brian's way of telling the world they really needed to come up with better questions.

"It's where people go to confess their sins. Or their fantasies. Mostly teenage girls declaring their undying love for the boy toy of the moment."

"And other people can read these confessions?"

"Yep. It's public. But it's also anonymous. There's a router in there that makes it difficult to trace back user names."

"Difficult, but not impossible."

"Nothing's impossible until I can't do it."

Jay lifted his mug. "I salute your arrogance."

"Look who's talking."

Jay smiled as he finished off his coffee, then handed the mug to Brian. "I'm going over to the computer for a minute. Bring me another cup."

Brian rolled his eyes. "Yes, master. Is there anything else you'd like? A foot massage, perhaps? A date with Penelope Cruz?"

"Yeah. I'd like to shut you up for once."

"You'd shoot yourself if you didn't have me to pick on."

Jay headed for the table. *Her* table.

He liked hanging out at the café, even though he

rarely used the computers. Conveniently, it was next door to his shop. And while the coffee was good, it wasn't the main selling point. He came here primarily for the women. All those beautiful NYU coeds, just dying to fling themselves at his big bad self.

But not her.

Damn, but he liked to see her blush.

When she first started coming to the café, he didn't even notice her. He didn't know who dressed her but, Christ, they needed to be drawn and quartered. She looked like someone's grandmother, with her cardigans and loafers. Except...

He couldn't remember now what had made him look at her. A sound she made, or a cough. Most likely, her blush. He'd been shocked as hell, that much he remembered clearly. She was gorgeous. Her skin was pale and flawless, delicate, like her body. Tall—he'd guess around five-seven or so—and a little too slender, she walked like a dancer. She'd smiled only once in all the months she'd been coming here. Not at him, but he'd caught it.

She was a natural beauty. No fake boobs, no fake hair, no piercings anywhere visible. She reminded him of someone from another time. The Renaissance, perhaps. But he also felt something else hiding behind those old-fashioned clothes, behind that blush. He knew it. He felt it. And he wanted it.

He sat down, ran his fingers over the keyboard. Was it his imagination or was there a trace of talcum lingering in the air? He turned on the machine and typed in the address for TrueConfessions.com. Once there, he checked it out, saw how it worked.

Good Girl.

That was the name he'd seen. If she hadn't been so flustered, she'd probably have blocked his view or turned off the computer. But she hadn't. And he was just the son-of-a-bitch to take advantage of the situation.

About five minutes later, just after Brian brought him another cup of coffee, he hit pay dirt—Good Girl's journal entries. He never did drink any of the coffee.

THE MUSIC from Tabby's bedroom reverberated through the apartment, the thundering bass making vases tremble and the crumbs on the table shift into interesting patterns. Amelia tried not to mind. At least, not too much.

Her roommates were nice girls, all three of them. A bit self-centered and obsessed with sex—but they were in their early twenties, so what did she expect?

Oh, please. While she hoped she wasn't quite so self-centered, she would be lying if she said she wasn't just as obsessed. Her roommates didn't help with that, either. Every one of them brought men home on a regular basis. Tabby had Josh, and they were the only two who were in a somewhat monogamous relationship. Donna rotated three guys, and for the most part, that worked smoothly enough.

Twice, though, two of her guys had shown up on the same night. Donna's solution? The *three* of them went to the bedroom. Amelia had had to use the ear-plugs that night. And the pillow over her head.

She'd been shocked, of course. For a while. Then, the idea of two men, two beautiful men, in bed with her, doing all manner of wicked things, made the idea almost appealing. Of course, Amelia would never have the nerve to do anything like that. She barely had the nerve to speak up in class, let alone flirt.

The thought made her blush, and her blush made her think of Jay. She closed her eyes to picture him better, and within moments she had to get a cold bottle of water from the fridge.

As she drank, she scolded herself. It was almost four-thirty, and she hadn't gotten back to her term paper. That meant she'd be in for a long night, which meant she couldn't go to the café in the morning. Or that she'd be so tired she'd probably fall asleep in class.

She wiped her mouth with a tea towel as her gaze moved to the dishes in the sink. She knew exactly how long they'd been piling up. Since the last time she'd washed them.

The others, especially Kathy, took advantage of her, she knew that. But she was also the only one of the four who seemed to have any time for the mundane things in life, like laundry and dishes and vac-uuming. Every time she cleaned up their mess, she swore it was the last time.

If she couldn't gather the courage to let her room-mates clean up after themselves, how on earth was she going to be strong enough to talk to *him?*

Right. Like that was going to happen. *And monkeys might fly out of my butt.* She chuckled, only slightly scandalized at herself. The *slightly* was because she'd been practicing. She'd said all sorts of bad things in the past two months. Curses that would make a freshman jock blush, insults that cut to the quick, and jibes so clever she had to laugh out loud. Of course, she'd only said them to herself, but hey, it was a start, right? Soon, she'd be just as brazen and hip as everyone else at school. Maybe not so crude, but she'd be in the ballpark. Not such a freak. An outsider.

She sighed as she leaned against the fridge door. Jay would never want a girl like her. Not in a million years. She should give it up. Chase him out of her thoughts. Forbid him to visit her dreams.

As if.

AT FIVE-FIFTEEN, Jay couldn't stand it another minute. He had to do something, and do it now. "Karl."

His assistant looked up from behind a vintage Harley. "Yeah?"

"How do you feel about locking up tonight?"

Karl nodded, then pushed his Buddy Holly glasses up to the bridge of his nose. The guy was older than Jay by ten years, but his long, scraggly hair and sparse goatee made him look like one of the students who came in here to drool. "You got a date?"

"Of sorts."

"No problem. Marie isn't gonna be home until after eleven."

Jay grabbed his jacket from the counter, shoved it

on, then picked up his helmet from the floor. "So she's still got that job?"

"Yeah. For some reason she likes working with numbers. Go figure."

Jay headed toward the door of his shop, his gaze automatically checking the display models, making sure the bikes were polished to a shine. "At least she's working."

"The second income is pretty welcome. Of course, if you'd pay me what I'm worth—"

"You don't want to go there, buddy."

Karl sighed like a lovesick teen.

"Get a grip."

His assistant laughed, but Jay had left behind the conversation as he pushed open the door. He'd hardly been able to think of anything all day...except Good Girl. At the café, he'd read a number of her early journal entries, and the more he read, the more intrigued he became. She came as a complete surprise to him—and that didn't happen often.

No one would guess that inside that Minnie Mouse of a girl lived a Jessica Rabbit woman.

He slipped his helmet on, then mounted his bike, a 1965 panhead, full dresser, electric glide, in mint condition. The engine came to life with a jolt, and then he was off, heading straight home to his computer, relaxing instantly as he listened to his bike purr like a kitten.

As he maneuvered through the Manhattan traffic, he kept picturing Good Girl peeling off her clothes piece by piece. But he had to cut that stimulating scenario short when he almost crashed into a hot dog vendor.

Twenty minutes later he pulled up to his brownstone. It was an old building, right in the heart of what used to be called Hell's Kitchen. The neighborhood wasn't what it used to be. It had been gentrified, with trendy shops and restaurants popping up like weeds. It didn't matter to him. They could build whatever the hell they wanted, as long as they left him alone.

He pulled the bike into a small alcove on the side of the building, and, helmet tucked beneath his arm, secured the bike with three sturdy locks. The neighborhood might be more upscale, but it was still Manhattan.

He headed for the door, pausing to nod at Jasper, the doorman. The guy was, like, a hundred-and-eight or something, and his uniform looked as if it had been made during the Crimean War. But Jasper had been the doorman for as long as anyone could remember, and that wasn't going to change until the old guy died. Not much about this building changed, including the fact that the elevator smelled like a wet dog. Jay lived on the fifth floor. The elevator stopped on three. The door slid open to reveal a man almost as old as Jasper.

"Jay, my boy. You're a sight for sore eyes."

Jay grinned. Shawn Cody was his neighbor, and the building busybody. If he'd been on three, it meant he'd checked up on Darlene, made sure she'd taken her meds. At eighty-four, Shawn was still sharp as a tack, and he kept tabs on everyone. He claimed to be a writer, but no one had seen anything he'd written. No matter. He was a good guy.

"How you doing, Shawn?"

The man sauntered in, and the wet dog smell was complicated by camphor and Old Spice. "As my father used to say, I'm as right as could be expected for a man destined to become dust."

"Not today, old man. Today, you're up and about and causing trouble."

Shawn nodded. "That's right. I'm here to comfort the tormented and torment the comforted."

The elevator resumed its creaky ascent, and Jay silently urged it along. If Shawn started talking, there was no escaping for a good ten minutes. But Jay liked the man, and his partner, Bill. They'd been together for almost fifty years. It hadn't been easy, but they'd stuck it out.

"You know," Shawn said, leaning back on his slightly humped shoulder. "I miss your granddad something fierce."

Jay nodded. "Me, too."

"He was a good fellow. A mighty good fellow."

"That he was," Jay said, the familiar sadness blossoming inside. His grandfather had passed away four months ago, and had been sick for a couple of years before that. Jay had taken care of him, and they'd grown close. So close, Jay had decided to stay on living in the apartment, even though he was the only one below retirement age in the whole damn place. It was cool. He helped out the old guys now and again. They were his grandfather's friends. Hell, his friends.

Not to mention the fact the apartment was rent controlled. For three hundred a month he had a two-bedroom place that most people he knew would kill for.

The elevator stopped on five, and Jay let the older man out first. "Take care of yourself, Shawn."

"The same to you, young man."

Jay headed down the dimly lit hallway. He opened his door, still expecting the scent of his grandfather's pipe smoke to waft over him. It didn't, of course. The pipe had been buried right alongside the man, per his request.

Jay took off his jacket and tossed it and his helmet on the couch. He grabbed a beer from the kitchen, took a swig, then went straight to the computer. A few moments later he was at TrueConfessions.com, reading the journal entries of one Good Girl, and the rest of the world faded to black.

2

The way he walks is sex itself. Not self-conscious, but sure. Arrogant. As if he knows. When he looks at me, my body aches with wanting him. But I'm not the woman he wants. I can't even smile at him, talk to him. I burn with desire, but I burn hotter from my cowardice.

JAY TOOK A PULL from his beer, only to realize the bottle was empty. As if coming out of a trance, he focused on the room, on the shadows playing against the wall. He stretched as he stood, releasing some of the tension in his shoulders. One more beer and then he'd stop. He had things to do. Nothing that was more interesting than Good Girl's confessions, but he still had to do them.

He opened the fridge, and the jar of Jiffy made his stomach rumble. Damn, it was after ten. How in hell had that happened? Skipping the beer, he grabbed the strawberry jam, bread and peanut butter. It wasn't fancy but it would do. And he could eat at the computer.

He put one sandwich on a paper plate and took a bite out of the other. As he stashed the food, he snagged the milk carton, then headed back to the living room.

Through the course of the night, he'd built a picture of Good Girl. Incomplete, of course, but still, she was clear to him. Bright, articulate, passionate and crippled by shyness. She wanted to break out of her shell, but she didn't know how. All she could do was write about her fantasies. Poor kid. She deserved more.

If only she could see how attractive she was. Stop trying to disappear into the woodwork. She even had a good sense of humor. A wry appreciation for life's ironies.

He clicked to the next entry and read as he ate.

So sex has a name. J.W.

Jay choked on his sandwich and spent the next few minutes coughing. J.W. had to be him, right? She'd been talking about him? Holy… *He* was the guy in her fantasies? *He* walked like sex itself?

Jeez. He'd figured she was talking about Brad Pitt. She'd mentioned the actor's name a couple of times, and it had never occurred to Jay…

This changed everything. Man. He shoved his remaining sandwich to the side of his desk and hunkered down. His gaze shot down the screen until he found her next entry.

I'm walking under the Washington Square arch. It's late. I should have been home hours ago. I hear footsteps behind me, and my stomach tightens, but come on, it's New York. When wouldn't I hear foot-steps? I keep walking, not looking left or right. Sud-denly, I'm slammed from the back and I cry out as I fall to my knees. A hand grabs my purse, and before I can see who he is, or even what he's wear-ing, he's off like a shot. But then, there's someone else, a man, chasing him. I watch, stunned, as the second man tackles the thief from behind. They're on the ground now, fighting, and I struggle to my feet. Before I take a step, it's all over, and the thief is running away, limping. The man who tackled him gets up, brushes off his trouser legs then looks at me.

He walks toward me, my purse in his hand.

It's him.

He holds out my bag. "I didn't know if you were hurt, or I would have gone after him."

"It's all right. In fact, it's extraordinary. You could have been killed, and you don't even know me."

He grins at me. "Oh, but I do know you, Amelia."

My heart pounds. Is this some trick? Some con?

"I've seen you in the café. And I know what you do on that computer."

"You do?"

He nods as he takes a step toward me. "I know all about you. What you like, what you want. What you need."

I can barely breathe. How is it possible? "What I write is private. Anonymous."

"I don't need to read anything," he says, as he reaches his hand to cup my cheek. "I read you,

Amelia. I see past all your defenses. I know how remarkable you are. I know how hard you've worked for your education. How much you care about your aunt. I know everything, Amelia. But mostly I know that you're the most incredibly sensual woman I've ever met. Every other man on earth is a fool, because they don't see it. They don't see you like I do."

I can't speak. How can he talk to me like this? We don't know each other at all...or do we?

He touches my cheek. Holds me captive with his gaze. Then his lips touch mine, and the rest of the world disappears. I'm drowning in his kiss as he folds me into the safety of his arms. His hands run down my back. He touches my waist. Then below my waist. He cups my behind and pulls me tight against his body. I feel his erection. It's huge!

Jay coughed, nearly choking on his beer. She thought he was huge? He looked down at his jean-covered half-hard cock. He'd never been ashamed to walk around in the locker room, but huge? Damn.

He went back to the story.

His kiss deepens, and then he pulls back. "Come with me," he whispers.

"Where?"

"To my bed."

"But—"

He puts his hand gently over my lips. "Don't

be afraid. You know you want this. Almost as much
as I do."

I nod slowly, knowing it's foolish to fight the truth.
He—

It ended. Boom. Just like that. Jay scanned the next
several pages, but the rest of the fantasy wasn't written down. What the hell? Why'd she stop just when
she was going to come to his apartment? When she
knew it was foolish to fight the truth—

He leaned back in his chair, shaking his head at his
own stupidity. It was a fantasy. Not a promise.

Yet.

AMELIA PUNCHED the time clock on her way out of
the library. Almost four, and she was done for the
day. She worked in the stacks, shelving and dusting.
It was a quiet world, perfect for her, even though the
pay was dreadful. She should go work on her term
paper, but all that was left to do there was a proofread,
and it might be wiser to wait for a day before she did
that.

Or was that just an excuse? Either way, she wasn't
going home. Not yet. She headed down Bleeker
Street, toward Washington Square and the café.
Would *he* be there? Her heart raced at the thought.
Just like it always did.

Her crush on him was ridiculous, she knew that.
But it was also the only thing in her life she was truly
passionate about. Except for her studies, of course,
but that was a totally different kind of passion. Jay

made her skin tingle, her stomach clench. She'd read a word somewhere, *limerance*. It meant that state of deep, addictive infatuation that happens when someone falls in love. She was absolutely there. Unequivocally. Shamefully.

Unfortunately, the man she was in limerance with didn't know her name. Thought she was a joke. And yet, as she neared the café, her pace quickened along with her pulse. She said her "Jay mantra." *Please, oh, please.*

Once she was at the door, she hesitated. Pushed her hair back, moistened her lips. Then she remembered how he'd almost touched her. Perhaps if he'd had a reason? She loosened a strand of hair by her cheek.

She walked in, instantly certain he wasn't there. The air was just air. Brian was at the bar, joystick in hand, making shooting noises as he destroyed enemy ships or some such. What an odd fellow he was. One would never guess his true age. He spoke like a teenager and played teenage games. On the other hand, he owned the café—and from what she could tell, it was a very successful venture. Two people were at computer terminals—the girl she'd seen before and a new guy. Young. A freshman, probably. They didn't look at her.

She walked over to her favorite workstation, but before she booted up, she took a couple of deep, calming breaths. It didn't matter that he wasn't here. Why should it? Even if he were, so what? He was out of her league, and she was out of her mind.

Her aunt Grace had told her many times that her

imagination was going to be the death of her. She shouldn't waste her time on daydreams. On wanting what she couldn't have. Aunt Grace might be a little extreme in her attitudes, but she had a point about the woes of an active imagination.

All of Amelia's problems were a direct result of wanting more than she could have. On the other hand, her aunt had been certain Amelia would never get accepted into the graduate program, or get financial aid. It had shocked them both when she'd won the fellowship. Full tuition, including books. It had been a miracle.

So who was to say there couldn't be a miracle here? Right?

She turned on the computer and logged in. She typed in the URL for TrueConfessions.com, and went directly to her journal entries.

What if I dropped something? And he picked it up? And our fingers touched. Sparks, electricity. Magic. Our eyes would meet and he'd smile, but not his regular smile. This one would hold surprise, would ask a question. I'd smile back in answer. Yes. My interest is real. Then he'd ask me my name. Sit at the edge of the table. See me. Not the blush, not the fear, but me. The part of me that is desire. That is passion. He'd touch my cheek and the caress would last, and it would stoke the flames inside us both. He'd lean over. Kiss me gently on the lips.

The front door opened, and her heart leapt. Only,

it was the other guy from the motorcycle shop. The one with the glasses.

She sighed, already feeling the foolishness of her fantasy. The loneliness.

Maybe I could say hello. That's all. Just hello. Would that be so earth shattering? Would the heavens fall and the oceans rise if I just said a simple hello?

Amelia stopped her fingers, stopped her thoughts, too. She didn't want to wallow in self-pity. Nothing bothered her more, and yet she found herself going there with alarming frequency. Again, it was clear that her problems were about expectations. Dreams that were too big for her little life. Quiet desperation.

No. That wasn't what she wanted. She wanted serenity. Satisfaction. Passion. Romance. Sex. Lots of sex. Mind-blowing sex.

She focused on the computer monitor once more.

I can't stop thinking about it. About making love. It's as if I have a compulsion, an illness, and the only medicine is two rounds with J. and plenty of water.

She smiled at that. Two rounds with Jay. When she couldn't even write out his name. What's wrong with this picture?

Maybe I'd be better off cutting my association with this place. If I never saw him, I'd forget about him. Maybe even become interested in someone else.

I could go out with the girls. They always invite me to their sorority parties, and I never say yes. That's it, of course. I'm going to go. I'm going to take a risk and see what happens. Who knows? It might turn out to be fun.

The line about the monkeys and her posterior came up again, only, this time it wasn't quite so amusing.

Why can't I get over this crippling shyness? What lesson am I supposed to learn, huh? To be brave? How can I be brave when I feel like I'm going to pass out? I hate this. I want to be someone else, anyone else. Donna or Kathy or Tabby. They all lead such exciting, wonderful lives. No wonder they leave the dishes for me. What else have I got to do?

She frowned. Not exactly her best attempt at cheering herself up. Before she could make things worse, she saved her work and logged off from the Web site. With forty minutes still to go on her time, she debated working on her paper, but decided instead to do something more uplifting. She typed in the address for her favorite online bookstore, and lost herself in page after page of book descriptions, knowing she could only buy one. She'd narrowed her selection down to three, when a shadow darkened her monitor.

Expecting Brian, she turned to find *him* standing not a foot away. Her heart slammed into her chest and she nearly pulled the mouse out of the computer.

"Did you drop this?"

She blinked.

"Miss...?"

Speak, dammit. Say something. Anything. "Edwards."

He smiled. Oh God. He smiled in a way he'd never smiled before. Sweet. Sexy. Her fantasy come to life.

"Did you drop this?"

She forced her gaze from his face to his hand. He held a ballpoint pen out to her. It was white with a blue cap, and she'd never seen it before. "No."

"Oh. I thought maybe you had."

She shook her head. "I don't have a pen like that."

His head tipped slightly to the side. "Would you like to?"

"Like to what?"

His grin broadened. "Have this pen?"

She blinked again.

He laughed. A lovely, rich sound that stirred something deep inside. It wasn't derisive at all. In fact, if she hadn't known better, she'd swear it sounded as if he found her...charming.

She reached out for the pen, her hand only trembling a bit, and when she touched it, his hand moved, brushing against hers, exactly as she'd imagined it a few minutes ago. Was she psychic? She'd never had a precognitive notion before in her life, but this...this was spooky.

"I'm Jay. Jay Wagner."

"I know."

"You do?"

She shouldn't have said that. Oh dear.

"And how do you know my name, Miss Edwards?"

"I've, uh, seen you in here. With Brian."

"Is that all? And here I was hoping you'd done a little digging."

"Me?"

He nodded.

"You must have noticed how I look for you every time I come in here."

"Me?" she asked again, feeling more and more like this had to be a dream. Nothing of this magnitude could possibly happen in real life. Not her life.

"Yes, you."

"Oh."

His gaze moved down, and she followed the glance to the pen, to both their hands still holding it. She let it go as heat filled her cheeks. At least there'd been a few seconds before she'd humiliated herself.

"I've never seen anyone blush so beautifully," he said, leaning over to put the pen on the table. And then his mouth was scant inches away, his warm breath fanning across the tender skin beneath her ear.

She froze. What was she supposed to do now? If she moved even a little, they'd touch. His lips... She couldn't faint now. She'd die. Only, she'd forgotten how to breathe.

"Amelia," he said, so softly she might have wished it. "I know who you are, Amelia."

Her heart stopped. The whole world stopped.

She felt his lips touch the shell of her ear. An almost-kiss. She quivered right down to her toes.

He pulled back, stood straight, captured her gaze. He didn't say another word. He just smiled before he walked away. To the door. Outside.

She collapsed. Not on the floor or anything. Mostly inside. Her heart resumed beating, her lungs filled with air, but she was boneless, weak as a kitten.

What in the world had just happened? Had she finally gone mad? Jay Wagner couldn't have... He wouldn't have...

Her gaze darted to the table. To the pen. Evidence! Then she turned quickly to the girl on the Power Mac. There. Proof. No one ever looked at her that way. She never made anyone jealous.

Okay, so it had been real. But how? Why? He'd known her name. He'd flirted with her.

It was flirting, she felt sure of that. Especially the whispering part. It was exactly the way she'd pictured it. Only a thousand times scarier. More wonderful. There had to be a fairy godmother floating around Washington Square, because this kind of thing simply didn't happen. She was Amelia. She was invisible.

Not anymore.

JAY WALKED INTO HIS OFFICE and slammed the door. He grinned as he sat down on his battered leather chair. Sliding down, he put one ankle over the other, crossed his arms and congratulated himself.

This was excellent. She was even prettier up close. Her perfume had knocked him for a loop, which was some trick, because the scent was as subtle as a rose behind a fence. Everything about her was subtle, almost hidden. The green of her eyes. The way her lips curved. The sound of her sigh.

It was like finding buried treasure. A far cry from the women he'd been with in the past few years. They'd mostly been into bikes, into leather, into hot, sweaty sex at four in the morning. Which wasn't a bad thing. But it sure as hell wasn't subtle.

Amelia Edwards would need a deft touch. Before she knew what to make of him, he'd have her in his bed. God, he wanted to see her naked. She was a mystery, and that appealed to him like no one's business. Shy as a fawn, delicate as a butterfly... And so filled with desire she didn't know which way was up.

He'd show her, all right. He'd take care of the education of Amelia, and he'd love every second of it. Damn, it was good to be a humanitarian.

He laughed as he rubbed his hands together, and he thanked the inventor of the computer and the wonderful folks who brought TrueConfessions.com to life.

He turned to his monitor, sitting proudly on top of two motorcycle manuals. Good Girl's latest entry still shimmered on the screen.

What if I dropped something? And he picked it up? And our fingers touched. Sparks, electricity. Magic. Our eyes would meet and he'd smile, but not his regular smile. This one would hold surprise, would ask a question. I'd smile back in answer. Yes. My interest is real. Then he'd ask me my name. Sit at the edge of the table. See me. Not the blush, not the fear, but me. The part of me that is desire. That is passion. He'd touch my cheek and the caress would last, and it would stoke the flames inside us both. He'd lean over. Kiss me gently on the lips.

He'd been damn close. Any more on the nose, and she'd have put two and two together. Which wasn't going to happen if he could help it. This was the best thing to come his way in months. Hell, maybe years. It was an adventure, and he felt his blood stir with the challenge. He felt alive for the first time in a long while.

The Amelia project would move to the next phase, as soon as he figured out what that was going to be. He needed her a bit off balance. So he'd wait. Even though he didn't want to. He'd wait.

In the meantime, he had all her fantasies to memorize. One in particular had kept him awake last night. An early entry, almost a year old. Only, he didn't believe she'd been coming to the café for a year. She must have used another computer. It didn't matter, except that the fantasy was about a biker. A man in black leather. A Harley. Was it a coincidence? Or had he simply not seen her back then? He'd asked Brian if he remembered, and his friend swore she'd only been coming there for five months.

If the fantasy predated her going to the café, it made things a lot more interesting. He'd stopped believing in coincidences a long time ago. Although he wouldn't admit it to anyone, especially his family, he believed there was a master plan.

Assuming it was a plan, how did he fit into it? Had she conjured him up? Or did she want him because he reminded her of her fantasy?

He wasn't going to figure it out tonight. He might never know, and that was no big deal. What did matter was that she wanted him, and he wanted her, and she'd never been on a bike in her life, and he was going to take her places she'd never dreamed about.

3

"YOU SURE you don't want to come to the party?" Kathy couldn't quite mask the pity in her gaze.

"No, but thanks." Amelia smiled, pretending the look was something else. "You know I don't mingle well."

"But you could learn. I think if you'd just let yourself, you'd do fine. Amelia, this is supposed to be the best time of your life. And you're spending it doing other people's dishes."

Stung, Amelia doggedly held on to her smile. "I'm not like you, that's all. It doesn't mean I'm miserable."

"Yeah, but aren't you lonely?"

She couldn't keep up the pretense any longer. Her smile faded along with her self-confidence. "Yes. I am. But it's not fatal."

"I'm not so sure about that."

Amelia walked over to the door of the bedroom she and Kathy shared. Her side of the room was immaculate. Kathy's was Martha Stewart's worst nightmare. "Hurry up. You're going to be late. And you've only tried on three-quarters of your wardrobe."

Kathy's gaze went to her own reflection in the mirror. She was gorgeous. Actually, all three of Amelia's roommates were beautiful. Kathy had pale blue eyes that flashed with humor. Her dark hair flowed to her shoulders, and she always knew how to make it look sensational. All that combined with her size-six figure—no wonder she had more men than she could handle.

As Amelia turned toward the living room, she heard the clunk of shoes hitting the floor. Kathy putting on wardrobe-change number five hundred.

The music grew louder as she walked past Donna and Tabby's room. Tabby, tall, stunning, with gently curved brown hair, was bent double, her hands flat on the ground, her knees locked. Not that her position was anything unusual. Tabby was the most limber creature Amelia had ever seen. They'd be chatting or watching TV, and Tabby would lift her leg straight up in the air and hold it there. It was amazing. All her men friends seemed to think so, at least.

Looking past Tabby, Amelia caught sight of Donna's reflection in the bathroom mirror. She had the mascara wand to her lashes and was patiently painting layers of dark black goo. It took her hours to do her makeup, which confused the hell out of Amelia. Granted, she wasn't one to wear makeup, but she knew the basic principals. There wasn't that much to do, considering Donna didn't have many flaws to begin with. She was the only blonde in the group. Petite with a ridiculously small waist, she was bright and funny and she had the best laugh. But on most days she was miserable, sure her world was coming to an end. Then she'd hook up with a guy, and poof— no more depression. Until the bitter end of the affair, complete with crying, moaning and vows of celibacy.

Living with the three of them made a great deal of sense financially. But Amelia would have preferred to live alone. All she saw when she looked at them was what she wasn't. Not pretty, not funny, not charming, not brave.

Not at all the kind of woman Jay would want.

The thought made her wince. She'd been battling this for two days now, trying to convince herself that what he'd said at the café was true. Only, it wasn't easy to believe. He was so gorgeous, so sexy. Any one of her roommates would look great on his arm. Amelia would just look odd. Everyone would wonder, What's he doing with *her?*

Her gaze went to Donna's bed, and the slinky top that lay over the pale pink comforter. Maybe if she dressed more provocatively…

Amelia picked up the shirt, then turned to the full-length mirror. It would be snug. Show off her figure, which was okay but nothing to write home about. But, who knows, maybe—

"Whoa, Amelia." Donna's laugh cut through the Foo Fighters, right into Amelia's heart. "Girl, you are not ready for that top."

Dropping the shirt as if it burned with the same fire flooding her cheeks, Amelia made a break for the door. Tabby stopped her with a hand on her shoulder.

"What top are you talking about?"

Donna went to the bed and held up the garment.

"What's wrong with that?"

"Nothing. Except, don't you think it's a little advanced?" Donna studied Amelia like something in a petri dish. "No offense, but don't you think you should try on some clothes that fit you, first? I mean, that are really your size?"

"You're right," Amelia said, forcing her voice to sound light, carefree, as if this wasn't the very reason why she didn't want roommates, why she didn't want anyone to get too close. "I was just kidding around."

"Hey," Tabby said. "Wait a minute. Donna's full of it. She's just selfish and didn't want you to borrow her top."

"That's not what—"

"It's okay," Amelia said, trying to cut the conversation off at the knees and make her escape. "You guys have a good time tonight. And don't get too drunk."

Tabby shook her head. "Amelia, you're so pretty. I wish you could see it. You've got the most gorgeous skin, and your body is to die for. You don't need to hide."

Not trusting her voice, she nodded, gave Tabby's hand a quick pat, then broke away. She went straight to the kitchen and turned on the water. Dirty dishes filled the sink and half of the countertop, and washing them seemed the safest thing to do. At least they wouldn't be able to see her cry.

Why did she have to be so sensitive? She wasn't a troll, she knew that. She had her pluses and minuses, like most women. But she'd been so painfully shy all her life that Aunt Grace's strict dress code had been a comfort, not a burden.

Donna didn't mean to be cruel. None of them did.

She thought of Jay. But not the way she'd been thinking since… No, this scenario had a new twist. What if Jay had been teasing her? Making fun of her?

She tried to dismiss the idea, but it sharpened as the moments ticked by. There was no reason on earth someone as gorgeous as Jay Wagner should be interested in her. She didn't know how to dress or wear her hair or do her makeup. He knew about her propensity to blush. He'd enjoyed embarrassing her before, hadn't he? This was probably a big fat joke to him. Watch the weird girl die of shame.

She sighed, wishing she could turn back the clock. She'd been so happy this morning when the possibilities seemed limitless. When she'd dared to dream her dreams.

She was a fool. A hopeless romantic. A dope.

What's worse, a broke dope. If only she could afford her own computer.

It didn't matter. She wouldn't go back to the café. Not ever. She couldn't bear the inevitable conclusion to this little farce.

JAY TURNED THE PAGE, scanning the *New York Times* as he drank his first cup of coffee. Nothing so far had piqued his interest except a piece about gas prices, but he continued. He wasn't much for routine, but this morning ritual was inviolate. As he skimmed the columns, he paused at a picture. Shit. It was his father and his brother, Peter, taken at a dinner honoring his father's illustrious career. Jay wasn't surprised he hadn't been invited.

His father, Lucas, was a big fish in a very small academic pond. A one-time poet laureate, he held the comparative literature chair at Cornell, and his books were always reviewed in the *Times,* although Jay knew precious few people who actually read them. Like his father, the books were pretentious as hell, with about as much warmth as a twenty-dollar hooker.

He read the full article and saw that his other brother, Ben, had also been in attendance. A fine time had evidently been had by all.

He folded the paper and finished his coffee, then went to get another cup. He studied his distorted reflection on his silver toaster, wondering if he should grow a beard. That would piss off the old man. But then, everything he did had that effect.

Jay took his cup into the living room, and, after he put the cup on the coffee table, sank down on the couch. It was stupid, this game he played with his father. Lucas wanted him to follow in his footsteps. Jay hated academia. A lose-lose situation.

Now Peter and Ben, they'd turned out as planned. Peter was an attorney with the most boring firm in New York, and Ben was an accountant. It had always been assumed that Jay would go to Cornell, like the rest of them. That he'd major in literature, and become a professor and writer. His grandfather had even set up a trust fund so that Jay wouldn't have to work during his graduate studies. Instead, Jay had bought the shop.

He looked at the bookcases that covered the wall to his right. Damn, he had a lot of books. Everything from Chaucer to Tom Clancy. And one very slim volume by a man named Jay Wagner.

Published when he was seventeen, the book, a coming-of-age story, naturally, had been reviewed by all the biggies. Not because he was a literary genius, but because of his father. *Kirkus Reviews* called Jay "The voice of his generation." *Publishers' Weekly* had hailed the book a stunning debut. Everyone wanted to know when the next book would arrive in stores.

Yeah, everyone including him.

He'd tried. He'd written pages and pages, enough for several novels—all of it crap. Whatever he'd had once, it was gone now. No amount of wishing or hoping would bring it back. In the almost ten years since *Damage* had come out, Jay had lost not only his talent, but his desire. He wasn't going to be a famous novelist. Or a famous anything. Which was a good thing. He loved his bikes, his friends, his women.

Amelia immediately came to mind, and he leaned back farther on the couch. She hadn't been to the café since he'd introduced himself. Brian and his part-time helper, Drew, had explicit instructions to call when she showed up. Jay had used his time wisely, going over screen after screen of her journal entries. Talk about writing talent. He wasn't all that keen on erotica, but this situation was another thing completely.

Picturing that prim, shy beauty as she'd written the most incredible fantasies had gotten him so hot he was surprised he hadn't burst into flames. Hell, picturing her living them out with him was more than any mortal could stand. He'd gotten so many erections in the past two days he'd had a tough time walking.

He'd given a great deal of thought to his next move. She'd provided him with a road map, and he intended to take every side trip necessary to get her in his bed.

He remembered one particularly vivid fantasy.

I see him across the room, standing by the exit, dark and dangerous in his tuxedo. He looks bored, as if nothing and no one has sparked his interest. His eyes meet mine, and his boredom disappears. He stares, unblinking, and I'm compelled to go to him. There is no choice, no decision. I barely see the room or the people around me. I stop an arm's-length away, and still that doesn't satisfy him. I move closer, and he cups my cheek, only it's not a tender move. He holds my head steady, staring through me, reading me.

He doesn't speak, doesn't need to. I belong to him now. I've abandoned my free will. His hand leaves my cheek and I wince at the loss. He smiles, understanding.

He leads me out of the room, to his car, a black Mercedes. I sit next to him quietly. We take off into the night, and I don't ask him where we're going. I don't ask him anything. Not his name or his intentions.

He touches my knee and I gasp, electrified. His fingers inch up my thigh. He rubs one finger over my panties, then stops. I spread my legs farther. He nods. Then he rubs me again. I can hardly breathe as his finger traces my cleft. He kills me with his measured pace, his even pressure. I try to buck forward, but he stops instantly. I understand. Through force of will, I remain still. Except for my heart, my pulse, my gasping breaths.

He pulls into a driveway, into a garage. Leads me inside, to a large living room with a crackling fire. His lips brush mine, teasing, and then he sits on the couch, waiting.

I know I must undress, and I do, slowly, my gaze on his. I don't stop until I'm naked, the firelight dancing on my skin.

He smiles, and I feel a rush of triumph. I'm not embarrassed, not burning with a blush. He likes what he sees. He stands, approaches me slowly, then touches my lip with his fingertip. I open my mouth, suck the finger in, swirl my tongue. He withdraws and touches my nipple. The wet from my mouth makes the nipple hard, hypersensitive. He runs a damp trail to the other nipple. So soft, so gentle, and yet I cannot move. He has me in his thrall, mesmerized. Aching. He will put out this fire inside me, but I must be patient. It's on his time, not mine.

A door slamming in the hall jerked Jay back to the real world. Damn. Two minutes of thinking about her and he was well on his way to another hard-on. He headed for the shower. Might as well get ready for work while he took care of business.

AMELIA STOOD OUTSIDE the café, her hand on the door. She shouldn't be here. She was just asking for trouble. It was very clear to her now that Jay hadn't meant anything he'd said. She was a joke to him. Of course. She'd been a fool to think otherwise.

Jay was gorgeous. Confident. Sexy. He could have any woman he wanted. Why would he waste his time on her? Not that she wasn't worth a man's attention, but the man for her would have to dig a little. See past her defenses. Past the walls she'd built around herself. Jay didn't need the bother.

She pushed open the door, resigning herself to whatever humiliation lay ahead. So he'd make fun of her. So what? She'd live. And dammit, she wasn't willing to give up her journal. Not for him. Not for anything. It was the one part of her life that was totally hers. Totally private. Of course, she could write in a bound journal, but she'd tried that before and it hadn't worked—she wasn't sure why. Maybe because she typed so fast. Almost as fast as her thoughts. She lost herself at the computer keyboard in a way she'd never experienced before.

If she'd had the money to buy even a used computer, she would have. But every penny was tight, especially since Aunt Grace wasn't doing all that well. If anything happened to her, Amelia would have to get back to Pennsylvania fast. Aunt Grace, like herself, had no one else.

Brian was behind the counter, and he smiled at her. Was he in on it, too? Probably. The place was busy, almost as bad as the day before midterms. None of the workstations were open, and if she had a smart bone in her body, she'd take that as an omen and get the heck out of here. Instead, she headed for the counter and a cup of coffee.

"The regular?" Brian asked. His gaze seemed suspiciously mischievous. As if he knew a secret. And she knew just what that secret was.

She nodded, trying to hide her blush by looking at the other side of the room.

"I can't tempt you to try something else today? No cappuccino? Latte? Hazelnut?"

She shook her head. "No, thank you."

"One plain coffee, coming up."

She didn't turn back until she knew he was busy with her order. They'd talked before. Plenty of times. But in the past he'd never given her a second thought. Like most men, he'd looked through her instead of at her. His change in attitude was all the proof she needed that Jay's attention was a joke. A cruel hoax. Oh God. She'd been so *gullible*.

"Here you go." Brian put her cup down. "Cream, sugar?"

She shook her head, then turned away from him, wondering if she should just leave the coffee and go. She'd find another Internet café. This was impossible.

"You know much about Jay?"

She turned so quickly on the stool that she nearly fell off. "Pardon me?"

"Jay. You know, the dude who owns the Harley shop next door."

"I know who he is. Why do you ask?"

"I was just curious. No reason. I've just known him for a long time is all."

"And?"

He shrugged and swiped at his unruly hair. "He's pretty cool. Smart as hell, too. Jay says he'll be somewhere, he'll be there."

"Thank you. I'll remember that."

He grinned again, and she noticed he had those clear braces on his teeth. Hmm. He was well into his thirties, and she didn't see many men his age with braces. Why was he telling her this stuff about Jay? Did he want her to feel even worse when she found out the truth? That didn't make sense. Brian might not see her as a desirable woman, but he appreciated her money. After all, she was a regular customer. So if it wasn't that, what was it?

She sipped her coffee, hardly tasting it as she juggled theories, none of them pleasing her at all.

"Uh, Amelia?"

Her train of thought derailed. He'd never called her Amelia. Or anything else for that matter. "Yes?"

"Don't take this the wrong way, okay?"

She cringed, wishing she had the nerve to throw her coffee in his face and run away.

"I've got this sister, see. And she went and got herself knocked up. Man, she's as big as a house. Anyway, she has these clothes she's giving away, and you look like you'd be about her size. I mean, the size she was."

Amelia blinked. Charity? He wanted to give her clothes? Did she look like a street person or something? Her clothes were a little big, but that wasn't a crime. Oh. Wait. Maybe he thought she wore clothes that were too big because she couldn't afford things that fit her.

Her cheeks heated in that cursed way, and she forced herself not to overreact. "That's nice of you," she said, her voice remarkably calm. "But I'm fine. Thanks."

"Sure. Yeah. Cool."

Mercifully, he walked to the other side of the counter to wait on someone else. Seconds later, the man at her favorite workstation got up, and she darted for his seat. With Brian's help, she'd made up her mind. She'd download all her work onto a floppy disk, and then she'd leave, never to return. What she couldn't decide was if it was enough to simply leave the café, or if she'd have to leave New York. Even living in the same state as Jay might be too horribly painful.

She logged on with shaking fingers and went to her journal site. She'd have to buy a floppy disk, which meant she'd have to talk to Brian again. Not yet. Not until she pulled herself together.

The front door opened, and all hope of composure

fled. Jay walked inside. Her heart fluttered, her stomach clenched, her cheeks reheated, and if she could have crawled into the disk drive of her computer, she would have. What had she been thinking? And why did she want him so badly? She closed her eyes, praying for Jay to ignore her.

"Amelia."

So much for prayers. She opened her eyes but she didn't look at him. "What—" She cleared her throat. "What can I do for you?"

He didn't answer, and finally she gave in and looked up at him. His face was a mask of concern. As if he cared. Right.

"Hey, what's going on?"

"Nothing that concerns you."

"Whoa. It must be bad." He snagged a chair from against the wall and brought it right next to hers. "Tell me."

"There's nothing to tell."

He sighed. "Okay. Have it your way."

"I intend to."

"But, surely you won't mind if I talk."

"Actually I have to—"

"I've just got this question I've been meaning to ask you."

She didn't want to know the question. She didn't want to feel this way just because he was near.

He leaned over and put his hand on her arm. His touch set off electrical charges that shot up and down her body. And it was only three fingers.

"I was wondering," he said, his voice much softer,

huskier, than a moment ago, "if you've ever been on a Harley."

"Pardon me?"

"A Harley-Davidson. It's a motorcycle—"

"I know what it is." She turned on him, her confusion overriding her embarrassment. "Why would you ask me that?"

He smiled that cocky grin she loved and hated. "I want to take you for a ride."

She opened her mouth, but, as was becoming something of a pattern, nothing came out.

"I see you on my bike. Your arms wrapped around my waist. I see you gripping the seat between your legs, feeling the vibrations. You'd like the wind, Amelia."

He scooted his chair closer, and the hand on her arm gripped her more tightly. She was incapable of turning away. His gaze had her rooted to the spot, his intensity blocking out the rest of the world. "I dreamt it. We're supposed to do this. We're supposed to take that ride."

She swallowed as she tried to calm her thundering heart. Either she was nuts, or he was. Because, oh my God, she'd dreamt the *exact same thing*.

4

————

DAMN, HE WAS GOOD. The look on her face was everything he'd hoped. Surprised...no, astonished, confused, vulnerable. Perfect. And oddly touching.

Funny how he felt as if he knew her more intimately than reading her journal should allow. Or maybe it was just the remnants of his youthful romanticism that spurred this sentimental streak. This was about sex, and he didn't want to forget that. And it wasn't just for his sake, either. Amelia needed help. She'd said it herself. She needed someone like him to set her free. Hell, he was doing her a favor.

"You saw me in your dream?"

He nodded, holding her gaze steady with his own. "It was the most vivid dream I've ever had."

She nibbled her lower lip. He wanted to offer his services in that regard, but that wasn't part of the plan. It would take all his determination, but he wasn't going to deviate, not an inch. Unfortunately, the longer he studied her face, the tighter his pants got.

He leaned forward, curious to see if she'd shy away. When he was near enough to feel her warm breath on his lips, her eyes closed and her lips parted.

He paused, his desire to keep going, to taste her, nearly breaking him. But at the last second, he remembered the larger goal. He jerked backward and jumped to his feet.

Of course Amelia's eyes snapped open, and her gasp made several people turn her way.

"I'm sorry," he said, taking a small step backward. "I had no right."

She reached out, touched the sleeve of his jacket for an instant, then pulled back. "It's okay. Honestly."

He shook his head. "No, it's not. I was out of line. You're not the kind of woman who—" He stopped. Took another half step back.

"Not the kind of woman who'd what?" she asked, her voice sharper, deeper.

"Who'd go off with a guy like me. That would be reckless. Crazy."

It was as if his words had pricked her ego, and she deflated before him. Her shoulders curved, her hand went to her lap, but what happened to her eyes made him wince. All the fire that had been alive in her green gaze a moment ago vanished, replaced with resignation and a sadness that was palpable.

He touched her hair. "I meant that as a compliment."

"Of course you did."

His fingers moved to her chin, and he lifted her face gently. "Amelia, come have lunch with me."

"What?"

"I want to talk to you."

"Why?"

The question caught him slightly off guard. Not because he hadn't rehearsed an answer, but because he wasn't quite so certain he was playing a role. "There's something about you." He shrugged. "I'm not sure what it is. Maybe the way you were in my dream."

Her soft pink blush made her that much more beautiful. Untouched, sweet. God, she must taste like honey.

"Why are you doing this?" she asked, her voice so soft he barely heard her. "It's not funny."

He sat down again, then took both her hands in his. The feel of her skin scrambled his thoughts for a moment, but a deep breath pulled him back. "I'm not trying to be funny, Amelia." He leaned forward a hair, and lowered his voice. "I'll tell you a secret. I don't like the coffee here. And I've got my own computer. But I come by almost every day. If you're not here, I move on."

She blinked, surprised, and he pictured her looking up at him as he made her come. As her mouth opened while she gasped with pleasure, her cheeks flushed, her hair a wild tangle on his pillows.

"I..."

Her little voice broke the spell, and he refocused. "What, Amelia?"

"I don't understand."

Something shifted in his chest. Just for a second— nothing major. He wasn't going all soft or anything. But his resolve strengthened and he knew he wasn't going to quit until this woman realized how beautiful she could be. "You're a pearl, Amelia. An undiscovered pearl hiding in your shell." He stood, held his hand out to her. "Please."

The poor kid looked scared to death. He wished she could see he wasn't going to hurt her. That this could be the beginning of something remarkable for both of them.

And maybe she did know that, because she stood and put her hand in his.

SHE FELT HIS STRENGTH through his fingers, his confidence when he led her to the door. He didn't let go of her—not when she walked outside, not down the block and around the corner. She had no idea where they were going, which should have been alarming, but it wasn't. Maybe she was in shock. Believing him had been so easy. It wasn't the words he used—although they were perfect—but the way he looked at her.

At first, she was just captivated by the deep, milk-chocolate brown eyes, the spiky lashes so thick they would have looked false on a woman. But their beauty was overshadowed by the concern she saw there, the earnestness.

He could be a con artist. Or he could be leading her down the garden path so he could humiliate her. Or he could have dreamed her dream, and this really was fate.

He stopped, and it took her a few seconds to realize they were at the Green Lips Café. She'd never eaten here, it was out of her price range—but she'd heard wonderful things about the food.

"After you," he said, holding the door open for her.

Her hesitation lasted only a moment. She'd eat macaroni and cheese all week if she had to. She wasn't going to back out now.

The decor inside was funky eclectic, with original oil paintings on the wall, all of them bright, odd, great. The waiters were young, and moving fast.

"Jay, good to see you."

A tall, elegant woman with short black hair kissed him on his cheeks European style. Jay smiled. "We'd like a table for two, Elaine. As private as you can make it."

Elaine shifted her gaze to Amelia, giving her a quick once-over, and Amelia wished she'd worn her coat. Her shapeless dress hung on her like a potato sack, and she felt ashamed. She shouldn't have come. She was out of her league in a world she usually tried to avoid.

But then he took her hand, and they followed Elaine through the restaurant. The woman was taller than Amelia, almost as tall as Jay. Her cropped pants hugged her slim hips, and her knit top showed off her figure. Kathy would have worn that outfit. Donna, too.

"Here you are," Elaine said, putting the large menus on a table close to the window. "Enjoy."

Jay pulled out a chair for her, and she sat, wishing she'd thought this through. She didn't belong here. But her self-castigation stopped abruptly when Jay took off his leather jacket. He wore a knit shirt, something old, like from the fifties. Short sleeves left his lower arms bare, and for that she was very grateful. He was so beautiful, so strong. His muscles flexed when he moved, and when he ran a hand through his unruly hair, she nearly whimpered. His chest. Oh my.

He sat across from her. She wished he was closer.

"The mussels are the specialty of the house," he said.

She bit her lip to stop from laughing. She could never have explained.

"But the ahi is always fresh and great," he went on. "If you're not into fish, they make a mean pasta primavera."

She ducked behind her menu. Everything was very expensive. The whole city was wildly overpriced, but she'd learned how to live on a strict budget. One meal here was worth a whole week of dinners. If she ordered an appetizer and a soda, she wouldn't completely break the bank.

Having made her decision, she put the menu aside, to find Jay staring at her. She abandoned herself to her blush. There was no use fighting it. She was just pleased her nervous reaction wasn't hiccups or flatulence.

"Would you like a drink? A cosmopolitan? Or a martini?"

"No, thank you," she said. "I'm not much of a drinker. I'd prefer a soda."

"Done." He signaled the waiter, and they ordered two sodas, and two appetizers—her pot stickers and his steamed mussels. Then, it was just the three of them—herself, Jay and the uncomfortable silence.

He didn't seem troubled. In fact, he looked satisfied, almost cocky. But then, when had she ever seen him when he hadn't looked that way? What gave him the confidence? It shocked her to realize she had a crush on a man she didn't know at all. It was only one step away from idolizing a rock star, which had always seemed foolish and a little pathetic. Was this any better? Taking a deep breath full of courage, she leaned forward and said, "Tell me."

"What?"

"Your life."

He laughed. "From conception or birth?"

"Birth is fine.

He laughed again, his rich baritone making her shiver inside. "I don't think we'll have time for my whole life."

"Okay, then. Tell me the important things. The things that shaped you."

His smile slackened as his gaze intensified. "You surprise me."

"I do?"

"Don't worry. That's a plus."

She didn't want to talk about herself. There wasn't much to say, after all. At least, nothing he would find interesting. But if she could get him talking, she could forget about herself. She might not be able to put two words together without blushing, but she wasn't afraid to ask questions. "Please?"

He leaned back in the wooden chair, clearly debating whether he would oblige. If he didn't, well, then, she'd deal with it, but she hoped it wouldn't come to that. Most people loved to talk about themselves. She'd used the deflection technique for years, and it never failed her. Once her companions started talking, she could relax. Not only did she feel more comfortable, but she learned a lot, too. It amazed her how people would go on if they weren't interrupted.

"All right. You asked for it."

She smiled, more relieved than she cared to think about.

"The important things," he said, mostly to himself. He'd taken a butter knife from his setting, and idly turned it over and over as his focus shifted to his past. "My mother died when I was eleven."

"How awful for you," she said, meaning it. She knew something about losing a parent.

He shrugged. "Yeah. It was. I liked her. She was pretty. Tall and slender, like you. People used to say she was a dead ringer for a young Lauren Bacall."

He glanced up at her, and she silently encouraged him to continue.

"I was raised in Ithaca along with my two brothers. My father wasn't around much. We had nannies."

"Plural?"

He nodded. "Oh, yeah."

"Three boys without a mother? You must have been a handful."

"I was."

"Only you?"

He nodded. "Typical black sheep. You know,

smoking, ditching school, firecrackers in the girls' locker room.''

''I'd like to say I can't picture it, but...''

''Just another rebel, like all the other rebels before me.''

''Are you still?''

He nodded. ''I suppose so.''

''In what way?''

He studied the knife. ''I, uh, had a pretty difficult time in school.''

''How?''

His expression changed to one she could only call wry. Maybe a little bitter. ''I had trouble paying attention.''

''ADD?''

''Nope. Boredom.''

''Really?''

He leaned forward, resting his arms on the table. ''I skipped a few grades. Went into a special school. Didn't make friends easily.''

She'd known someone with a very similar past. ''How high is your IQ?''

His eyes widened in surprise.

She must have hit the nail on the head. ''Come on. 'Fess up. I won't make fun of you.''

''That's what they all say.''

''Jay...''

He sighed again. ''Around one-ninety.''

''Wow.''

''Not all it's cracked up to be, I assure you.''

"Did you excel at everything? Or did you special-ize?"

His gaze narrowed. "I was about ten miles off about you, wasn't I? You aren't in the least bit shy."

"Oh, but I am."

"I was kidding. What I didn't know about was this—"

"What?"

"Determination? Curiosity? I don't know what to call it, except unexpected."

Her cheeks heated. "Okay, back to you."

"Relentless." He gave her half a grin. "I like that in a woman."

"Okay, so you can make me blush. Don't pat your-self on the back too hard. Mr. Yamahara at my local grocery makes me blush, and he can't speak En-glish."

"Point taken."

The waiter came with the drinks and food. For the next few minutes, they concentrated on the appetizers. She decided she was crazy about the restaurant, but her focus returned to Jay. He even ate sexy. His jaw muscle flexed with each bite, which wasn't nearly as distracting as the way his lips glistened with a touch of oil from the pot sticker dipping sauce. She wanted to lick it off him, right here, in the middle of the café.

"Now, that's something," he said.

"What?" she asked, jerking her gaze from his mouth.

"You just blushed again. And I haven't said a word."

She touched her cheeks with her fingertips. "Maybe I'm allergic to something in the food."

"Or maybe you were having blush-worthy thoughts."

She grabbed her soda and tried to hide behind the straw.

"I saw you looking at my mouth."

"I wasn't."

"Amelia. I'm surprised at you."

"Okay, I was. It wasn't a big deal."

He leaned in again, and her body went on full alert. How he did that to her was a mystery. It was like an electrical field had been breached, the very air changing its chemical components. "I think when it's my turn to ask the questions, we'll find out exactly how big a deal it was."

She cleared her throat, knowing she was adding fuel to the flame by blushing right down to her toes. There was only one solution. "But it's not your turn. It's my turn, and you haven't answered my question."

"Which was?"

"Were you a prodigy?"

He stared at her for a moment, no expression on his face, his gaze a bit glassy, and then he was back. "Yeah, I was."

"Math?"

He nodded. "It started out that way. Then I got interested in writing."

"That's unusual."

"I suppose."

"Poetry? Or prose?"

"Both."

"What about music?"

"What about it?"

It was her turn to lean in. "Come on, Jay. You know math and music are connected. And that most prodigies tend to be great in both."

"Are you a teacher?"

"No. But I know something about the subject."

"How?"

"I had a friend who was like you. She died when she was seventeen."

"I'm sorry."

"Me, too. She was wonderful."

He looked away for a few seconds, and when he looked back his demeanor had shifted again. He was like a chameleon, changing his colors with his mood. "Do you want to order?"

"No. I'm fine."

"Are you sure?"

She nodded. "But you go ahead."

"I'm not hungry anymore. Besides…"

Amelia's chest tightened, although she couldn't say why. His tone, the wicked gleam in his eye, perhaps. "What?"

"I owe you a ride on my Harley."

In the blink of an eye, the easy confidence that had marked their conversation disappeared. She didn't want to go, and she wanted desperately to go.

"Come on," he whispered. "We know each other now."

"No, we don't. I know some things about you. That's not *knowing* you."

"Okay, then, ask me."

"Will you tell me the truth?"

He nodded, crossed his heart with his index finger. "Shoot."

Amelia held her breath as a dozen questions popped into her head. But there could really be only one. "What will you do with me," she asked, "at the end of the ride?"

5

JAY WASN'T PREPARED for her question. Especially after the surprising nature of their conversation. He'd thought he had her pegged. He knew a lot about women, and while they occasionally veered left when he figured they'd veer right, Amelia had hung a U-turn.

He'd assumed he'd be the one asking the questions. Drawing her out. Wrong on both counts. Her intuition was just this side of scary, and the way she looked at him while he talked—it reminded him of how he focused on a particularly complex physics equation. Not that he'd done that in awhile, but that intensity wasn't something easily forgotten.

It didn't change anything, really. He would stick to the program, play it out till the end. It would just be a hell of a lot more interesting.

"Do you even know?" she asked.

He nodded. "Let's just say I know what I'd like to do with you."

"What would that be?"

Was she flirting? Egging him on? Totally naive? He honestly didn't know. It was a unique situation, with a unique person. Her writing had clued him in to her intelligence, but he hadn't seen the whole picture. The only thing that did make more sense now was the nature of her fantasies. All that passion had to be channeled somewhere. With luck, it would be aimed his way. What the hell.

"I'd like to make love with you."

She disarmed him completely with a look of innocent shock. When had he ever been with a woman like her? He had to be careful not to push too hard. He took her hand and gave it a reassuring squeeze. "But I know it's too soon for that."

"No, that's not the issue."

Could have fooled him. She'd turned white, her eyes had grown huge, and her fingers had gone to the top button of her blouse. "What is the issue?"

"You're very good-looking."

He choked back a bark of laughter. "Thanks."

"I mean it. You're gorgeous, and you know it. So does every woman you meet. So why me?"

"*I know it?* What do you mean, I know it?"

Her shoulders relaxed a bit as her color returned. "I thought we were talking about me now."

"Right. Sorry. I'll get back to you in a second, okay?" He turned before she could respond, and stopped their waiter. "Scotch, neat."

"And for the lady?"

"Another soda, please."

He nodded, then headed for the kitchen. Jay cleared his throat and turned back to Amelia. She looked like a kindergarten teacher in her white starched blouse, her sweater concealing anything of interest above or below her waist. Her skirt touched the bottom of her kneecaps, and while he hadn't paid much attention to her shoes, they sure as hell weren't stilettos. Yeah, her face was pretty. More than that—she had an ethereal quality that mesmerized him. But even that wasn't the reason he wanted her as he did.

It all boiled down to the dichotomy. That prim and proper exterior hiding a wildness no one would ever imagine. And he'd seen it. He hadn't been kidding about the fate thing. Why else would the opportunity have presented itself?

He leaned toward her again and didn't speak until he'd captured her gaze. "I don't know," he said. "I'm not being flippant. It's got me confused, too."

Her lips curved into a delicious pout.

"Hear me out." He touched her wrist with his fingertips and rubbed the soft skin. "I see something in you. Something that I have in myself, I guess. Something you try like hell to hide."

She pulled back, turned her head, but he wasn't going for it. Gently, he guided her chin around until their eyes met.

"I don't know what you're talking about," she said, her voice tight, frightened.

"Yes, you do. I know you do. I see it in your eyes. I feel it when I touch you. There's a passion inside you that's going to eat you alive if you don't do something about it. It's been dormant too long, and I don't think you can take much more. Why should you? You're a sensual woman. No matter how many sweaters you put on, you can't hide that."

She let out a long, slow breath. "So, what you're saying is, I'm your good deed for the week? Give the repressed girl a thrill?"

He shook his head. "No. Not at all. I've been watching you just as long as you've been watching me. Tell me you don't feel this heat between us and I'll walk out the door and never bother you again."

She opened her mouth, then closed it again.

He held back a smile. "I don't know what's going to happen between us," he said. "But I'd like to find out."

Her gaze broke from his. "I'm not the kind of woman you're used to dating."

"How do you know?"

The look she gave him was enough to shut him up. "I'm different," she said. "I know that. I'm not hip, if you even call it that, I don't like crowds, I'm—" she cleared her throat "—not very good at this."

"I don't agree. You're very good. Because you're telling the truth. I'm not out to hurt you, Amelia. Or scare you. I'm following my instincts. There's something to this, I know there is."

"What does that mean? What do you want?"

"I want to spend time with you."

"In the bedroom?"

He nodded. "Eventually. But for now, I just want to talk. To listen."

"I don't know…"

"I do. Let's just give it a chance, okay? A week. If you still feel this way next week, then fine. I'll never darken your door again."

She studied him carefully, her green eyes filled with equal parts fear and intelligence. "All right," she said finally. "We'll try it for a week."

He smiled. Big time. "This is gonna be a hell of an adventure, Amelia."

She shook her head. "That's what I'm afraid of."

He touched her cheek with the back of his hand. "Don't be afraid," he said. "I won't hurt you."

"Promise?" she asked in a young girl's voice.

"I promise." Then he stood, pulling her up with him. Right into his arms. He kissed her cheeks, her nose. Her lips.

And he knew, right then, that he was in trouble. Serious trouble.

AMELIA SAT ON THE EDGE of her bed, her gaze unfocused, thinking about her lunch with Jay. It felt more like a dream than anything else. Men like Jay didn't happen to women like her.

Could he possibly be for real? Oh, she hoped so. Wouldn't that be something? Especially now that she knew so much more about him. His intelligence didn't surprise her, somehow, and she wondered if that had anything to do with Mary, her tragic friend who'd died so young. Mary had been a quirky girl, who had a great deal of trouble adjusting to the world. She grew bored so easily, her mind flitting from one topic to the next. Sometimes it had been hard to keep up with her. But when she did slow down and direct her formidable concentration toward one thing, it had the same kind of intensity that she felt from Jay.

Amelia wasn't nearly bright enough for him. She doubted many would be. And, unlike Mary, Jay's persona was strong, confident and incredibly sexual.

She took off her sweater and caught sight of her reflection in the mirror. Okay, yes. She did dress like someone's maiden aunt—but what was she supposed to do about that? Clothes cost money, and she barely had enough to make ends meet. She wondered, if money weren't an issue, would she find some other excuse? He was right. She did hide in her baggy skirts and sweaters. It had always been comfortable. Until now.

For the first time in years, she wanted to be a part of, instead of apart from. She wanted to be pretty, sophisticated, brave. Which, unless there was a fairy godmother somewhere in her future, wasn't going to happen.

Jay's interest in her did give her pause, however. He saw something in her that she didn't see. Something attractive, or else he wouldn't want to make love with her.

She stepped out of her skirt, took off her blouse and bra, and slipped into her sleep shirt. It was only eight-thirty, but she wanted the privacy of her bed. None of the roommates was here, but that could change any moment, and they wouldn't disturb her if she was under the covers.

First, though, she had to take care of the mundane, like folding her clothes, brushing her teeth, washing her face. She raced through her tasks, unable to stop thinking about Jay. About making love.

Finally, she was through, and after turning out the light and shutting the door, she climbed into bed and closed her eyes. Of course, she pictured Jay—only now, there were details. She remembered his scent— masculine, slightly spicy. The way his fingers made her skin tingle. Mostly, though, she remembered his lips.

She'd never been kissed like that. Never. Gently, at first, but not timidly. Not at all. He'd held her tight, his hard body pressed against hers, making her knees wobbly and her heart pound. He'd given her a moment to get used to him, to relax—although she hadn't. Couldn't. Especially not when his warm, wet tongue touched the crease of her lips. She'd gasped, and he'd taken advantage of the moment, slipping his tongue inside.

Amelia squeezed her legs together, but it wasn't enough to ease her growing tension. Turning to her side, she slipped her hand inside her panties.

As she remembered in exquisite detail how he tasted, how he'd explored her so sweetly, how he'd known just what to do, her excitement grew until she breathed hard, fast, and her body grew taut as she climbed to her release.

Then her orgasm swept everything in the world away except sensation and memory. Suspended in a cocoon of pleasure, she whispered his name. Let herself believe that her dreams could come true.

Taking in deep, slow breaths, she struggled to regain her equilibrium, which wasn't easy. She'd actually kissed him. For real. In public. He'd touched the top swell of her behind, his chest had rubbed against her breasts, and he'd said he wanted to make love to her. Said it out loud. Said it with a look of raw desire in his eyes.

He'd seen past her fortress. The one thing she'd always wished for someone to do, and had never expected to see. He understood the heat inside her, the urges that were so strong she thought she might go crazy.

She'd promised him a week. She didn't want to spend that week worrying that it all might be a practical joke, or worse. She didn't want her insecurities to ruin everything. It would all be over soon enough.

So she made a decision. A vow. For the first time in her life, she was going to be the woman she tried to hide. Instead of writing her fantasies in secret, she'd live them. She'd let go of her fears, her shaky past, and dammit, she wouldn't let her cursed shyness stop her. Not this time. Because if she failed, if she let the fear win, she might never try again.

JAY SLAMMED HIS BOOK CLOSED and headed for the shower. He'd been trying to read for over an hour, and so far he'd read one sentence about fifty times. It wasn't even a good sentence. It was Amelia, of course. Only this morning, he'd been so sure he had everything figured out. *Right.*

The conversation at lunch had been confusing enough, but when he added the kiss—

That kiss. It had taken him by surprise. Not her lips—he'd known they'd be soft and lush. Not her heat. Not her. He'd been blown away by his reaction. Yeah, he'd wanted to have sex with her the moment he read her first fantasy, but now he had to have her. Unequivocally. Failure was not an option.

But he also couldn't be a shit.

How had she known about his IQ? No one knew that except for his family. He made a point of keeping the information to himself. All it did was make people uncomfortable. Even Karl had no idea. Yet, she'd picked up on it within the first half hour.

He hadn't lied to her. Not really. Now that they'd talked, now that he'd touched her, his altruism had taken a back seat to his lust. It wasn't a noble emotion, but it was honest. The woman intrigued the hell out of him. He had to see what was under those clothes. He needed to see what she'd be like when she let down her guard.

He turned on the shower and undressed, sighing as he released his semi-hard cock from the confines of his jeans. Rubbing it briefly, he climbed under the hot water and closed his eyes. Now he could pay proper attention. He fisted his erection, ready to come quickly, wash his hair and get to bed. Only, Amelia wasn't going with the program.

He kept thinking about how she'd studied him with those green eyes of hers. He wasn't sure what she saw, but he knew yearning when he saw it. She wanted him, which was a damn good thing because he wanted her something wicked. When she'd nibbled her bottom lip, it was all he could do not to take her on the table—the hell with the rest of the customers.

But there was an element of weirdness, too. On the one hand, she sparked something in him, a feeling of safety, as if he could tell her his secrets. On the other hand, she made him hard in the blink of an eye.

He sighed, knowing he was trying to fathom the unfathomable. He might be a genius, but come on, he didn't know squat about women. No one did. But he most especially didn't know about this woman. Amelia in hiding. Walking around in that clever disguise of hers, trying to disappear from view. Which gave her an excellent place from which to watch. Right in the thick of things, but not there.

Enough with the psychoanalysis. He pumped his hand, getting into a nice, easy rhythm. He had to be inside her. To feel her energy surround him. He'd wanted plenty of women in his life, for any number of reasons, most having to do with sex, but this was different. She was different. He wanted to unwrap her like a present, tear away the facade and see what lay beneath. And once he had her naked and open, he'd milk all that passion, all that slow, simmering sexual tension, and he'd take her to the moon. She'd scream for him before he was through.

He thought about one of her fantasies. In it, she'd gone to a man's house on an innocent errand. And while she waited for him, she happened to catch his reflection in a hallway mirror. The thing was, he was naked. Completely naked. And like Jay, he was using his hand to get some release. In Amelia's fantasy, he caught her staring, then smiled. She'd walked slowly down the hall, and when she arrived in his room, looking at him in all his hard splendor, she'd silently sunk to her knees and taken his cock in her mouth.

He closed his eyes, sharing her fantasy, but from a different point of view. About two seconds later, he shuddered as his climax hit. As he whispered her name.

SHE NEEDED NEW UNDERWEAR. Not white, not sturdy, not practical. She needed silk and lace, soft pink and red hot. The problem was, sexy underwear cost money, which she didn't have.

Her gaze went over to the closet. Tabby's clothes were gorgeous, including her underwear. Of course, Amelia couldn't borrow those—but what about a pair of jeans? Tabby had offered to lend her clothes many times, and she'd always refused. She'd never even tried anything on.

But she wasn't the old Amelia today, was she? She was the new, improved, impossibly brave Amelia. She pulled the jeans from the hanger and slipped them on underneath her nightshirt. The pants were too long, and a little too big.

Before she could change her mind, she marched straight over to the other bedroom and knocked on the door.

"Come in."

Kathy was still in bed, and Donna was in the bathroom. "I have a favor to ask," Amelia said.

Kathy yawned. "Shoot."

"I need to borrow some clothes."

Kathy's mouth closed with a click of teeth. "Somebody call the *New York Post*." She threw back her comforter and climbed out of bed. "Girl, it's about damn time."

"I was thinking jeans."

"Jeans? We got your jeans right here." Kathy went to her closet and pulled out a pair of faded Levis. Then another pair, darker this time, and still a third pair that had flared legs. She tossed them at Amelia, who managed to clutch them before they fell to the floor.

She put them on the bed, took off Tabby's pants and tried on the Levis. A little snug, but then, jeans were supposed to be snug. Only, they were too short by a good couple of inches.

"Nope," Kathy said. "You look like you're waiting for the flood."

Amelia laughed, but it was more about nerves than humor. She really was doing this. It felt like she was trying on costumes, but she didn't care.

Another pair of jeans hit her on the shoulder before pooling on the floor. She picked them up. They were Donna's. "I don't think so," she said.

"What?"

"I don't think Donna wants me wearing her things."

"Hold on." Kathy walked to the bathroom door and banged on it.

"What?" Donna's muffled voice sounded irked.

"Amelia's going to borrow some clothes."

"*What?*"

"You heard me."

"Which clothes?"

"Who cares. As long as they don't belong to her."

"Fine," Donna said. Then the door opened a crack and she stuck her head out. "What's the occasion?"

Amelia shrugged. She didn't want to tell them about Jay. Or about her resolution. "I just feel like it."

"All righty, then," Donna said, and Amelia noticed she had one eye made up and the other bare. "Go for it. Just don't ruin anything, okay?"

"I'll do my best."

Donna shut the door, and Amelia turned to Kathy. "Do you have class today?"

"Not until two."

"Do you think you could help me with my hair and some makeup?"

Kathy's brows raised and she broke into a wide grin. "You got it, toots. But let's get the wardrobe down first. This is so cool."

Amelia took off the ill-fitting jeans. She wasn't sure about cool. Scary? Oh, yeah. But cool? She pulled on Donna's jeans. They felt good. Snug, but she could still breath. And they were long enough. But still...

She walked over to the full-length mirror, grabbed her sleep shirt and pulled it off. She tossed it to the bed beside her, then stared at her reflection. She had a figure. Of course, she'd always known she had a figure, but she hadn't realized she had a *good* figure.

"Holy shit, kiddo," Kathy said. "You're incredibly phat."

"I am?" She put her hands to her waist. "I'm your size."

"Phat. Not Fat. Spelled P-H-A-T. Or something like that. It means you look great."

Amelia turned to her roommate. "Really?"

Kathy nodded. With a gentleness Amelia had never seen before, Kathy leaned over and kissed her cheek. "You're gorgeous, Amelia. You'll knock 'em dead."

"I hope so," she whispered.

Kathy, done with her little Kodak moment, went back to the closet and started pulling out tops.

6

JAY TAPPED HIS FINGERS on the counter as he waited for the credit card machine to spit out the receipt. It was a good sale, without financing, which would, under normal circumstances, make his day. But circumstances weren't normal.

He was obsessed with Amelia.

Not to the stalker stage or anything that ominous. Just to the point that it drove him crazy.

His plan of attack had to be carefully staged. He didn't want to spook her. She was like a doe in the wild. Curious but skittish. He needed to make her feel safe enough to expose herself, and not just her body. She needed to be comfortable enough to turn her fantasies into realities. For a girl as shy as Amelia, that was going to take some time.

He'd always been a patient man. At least, when it came to women. Hell, most of the time, the women did all the work. Not that he was God's gift or anything, but the quieter he got, the more the ladies seemed to want him. He'd never understood that until now. The shoe was on the other foot, and he was the one in pursuit. He'd take what he'd learned and use it to win Amelia over.

The credit card machine came to life. His customer, a plumber from the Lower East Side, signed the paper, and Jay walked him outside to his new bike. It was a beauty—a fully loaded Night Train in Jade Sunglo Pearl. They shook hands, and Jay watched him roar down the street. Business had been good lately. He'd been able to put aside some serious cash and make some solid investments. He would never have made this kind of dough if he'd done what his father had wanted.

He went back inside. There were bills to be paid, orders to go over. Karl was there to take care of any customers, so Jay went straight to his office. Forcing himself to put thoughts of Amelia on the back burner, he bent to his tasks, and didn't come up for air until he heard Karl say his name.

"Jay, someone here to see you."

Jay nodded as he saved his file on the computer. A quick glance at his watch showed he'd been at it for about an hour, but it had been a productive hour. Only eleven, and he'd gotten through almost half of his In box.

He ran a hand through his hair as he walked into the showroom. Whoever wanted to see him wasn't at the counter. Wasn't in the shop.

"She went outside for a minute," Karl said. "She'll be right back."

"She?"

His assistant nodded.

Interesting. Jay hadn't been going out much lately. It might be Giselle. They had a strictly physical relationship which they renewed every time she was between boyfriends. Or it could be Annie. The blonde from the Bronx. She'd worn him out on several memorable occasions.

Of course, it could just be a customer. Whoever it was, she must not have wanted to see him that badly. The minutes ticked by, and then a call came in from a collector in Connecticut and Jay forgot about the mystery woman.

A few minutes later, he had a manual out on the countertop and was searching for the engine specs on a 1934 VLD, when he noticed her legs. Sweet. Snug Levis hugged fine hips and a small waist. The sweater she had on, a deep purple, did what sweaters were meant to do: show off a gorgeous pair of breasts. His gaze moved up to the long, dark hair draped over her shoulders. He smiled. This wasn't one of his women. And if he weren't occupied with thoughts of Amelia, he would have done something about it. He looked up those last few inches.

The phone slipped from his hand. He barely registered the clunk. He was too busy being totally blown out of the water.

Amelia wasn't hiding anymore.

HER FACE BURNED with a blush, and she could only sneak peeks at his face. She'd been relatively calm on the way over to his bike shop, but now that she was here standing in front of him, Amelia felt positively naked.

Her roommates had worked on her until late last

night, experimenting with clothes, makeup and hair.
She'd felt like a Barbie doll at a slumber party. She'd
struggled hard not to run away, even though every
instinct tried to propel her. And when she thought
about who she was doing this for, it was doubly difficult.

She dared another glance at Jay, but she couldn't
read him. His mouth hung slightly open, his eyes
were wide and unblinking, and totally confused. "It's
me," she whispered. "Amelia, from next door."

He exhaled, shook his head. "I thought I knew who
you were," he said, "but now I'm not so sure."

She had no clue what to say. Or what to do with
her hands. He just kept staring at her like she had two
heads or something. Surely a change of wardrobe
couldn't be that shocking. She was still Amelia, and
still plagued by her awful shyness, and Jay wasn't
helping matters.

"They're not mine," she blurted out. "I borrowed
them. Because I thought... Well, you said about the
ride. Maybe we could, you know... Today, I mean.
But you're busy, so never mind. Sorry to bother
you." She turned and headed for the door.

"Amelia wait."

She wanted to, but her feet kept going. She made
it all the way to the door before he captured her arm.

"Wait."

Despite the fact that a heart attack was imminent,
she didn't try to break free.

"Hold on, okay? I need a minute, here."

"I'm still just Amelia."

"Right. Like a Bengal tiger is still just a kitty."

"Is that a good thing?"

After a moment of dodge-and-parry, he caught her gaze and held it. "I think you're even more beautiful than yesterday. And yesterday, you knocked my socks off."

Warm pleasure filled Amelia from the inside out. "Oh."

"Yeah. Oh."

"Uh, boss?"

Jay turned toward the counter and his assistant. "What?"

Karl held up the phone. "You gonna call Jim back, or what?"

"Oh. Yeah. Tell him I'm sorry. I'll call him later. Probably tomorrow."

Karl nodded, gave Amelia a puzzled look, then went back to the phone. She'd seen him in the café a lot, although they'd never been introduced. He seemed very nice, if a bit peculiar. He reminded her of a Labrador retriever, kind of galumphing through life.

Jay turned back, and thoughts of Karl vanished from her mind. Now that she knew the wide-eyed wonder on Jay's face meant he liked what he saw, she felt giddy with relief. No man had ever told her she was beautiful. Not like this, at least. Kevin, the only boy she'd dated in college, had called her pretty, but his wandering gaze made her question him. It hadn't mattered if they were deep in conversation or in the middle of an argument, if a really beautiful girl walked by, he'd watch the stranger with a hunger she never saw when he looked at her.

Jay had that hungry look right now. And there was no one else in sight.

"What were you saying before?" he asked.

"Oh. About…well, you'd asked if I wanted to go for a ride, and I thought, maybe…"

He smiled. "Let me get my jacket. You wait right there."

"Okay."

He cupped her face with both hands and kissed her on the lips.

She gasped, caught off guard. It wasn't a kiss like the one the day before—slow, sensuous, meant to stir things up. This was firm, quick, a dart of his tongue. A kind of exclamation point. A moment later, he was halfway to the back of the shop, chuckling as he walked—and she remembered how to breathe.

"WHO IS THAT?"

Jay looked up as Karl entered his office. "You've seen her before. She hangs out next door. She's always at that corner workstation."

His dark brows furrowed. "I don't think so. The only person I ever see there is that baggy girl."

Jay smiled. "She is the baggy girl."

"Get outta here."

Jay locked his desk drawer, then looked around the office for anything he might need. "I don't think I'm going to be back today."

"No, really?"

"Get your mind out of the gutter. We're going for a ride upstate, that's all."

"Right." Karl grinned. "A ride. I've heard that before."

"This is different." Jay paused, realizing the truth of his words. It *was* different. He'd known she was beautiful, and that somewhere underneath those awful clothes there was a decent body. He hadn't guessed that she'd be so...tasty-looking.

She wasn't model thin, and that was the whole key. She was a woman, with womanly curves, and he could imagine clearly how soft she'd be in his bed. Maybe that's why she tried so hard to hide. With a figure like that, any guy past puberty would want her. Add to that her innocence mixed with that single-minded focus, and what you got was a woman straight out of every man's fantasy.

He chuckled at the irony.

"What's so funny?"

"Nothing. You're good, right?"

Karl nodded. "I'll be here."

"Cool. Sell some bikes, would you?"

"Yes, sir."

Jay walked around his desk, slipped on his jacket, and headed for what promised to be a very interesting day.

Amelia had stayed where he left her. The light from the glass windows gleamed in her hair, and he lost several IQ points as he took her in. Mentally pushing Karl out of the gutter, he claimed the territory for himself. Damn, she was fine. And all her X-rated fantasies were about him. He felt unworthy. Not that he wasn't going to take advantage of what he knew, of course, but he was humbled.

However, he had a more pressing problem. Literally. His penis clearly had no concept of appropriate timing. As he walked toward her, snippets of her journal tormented him. How was he going to survive two hours on a bike, with those legs wrapped around him? With those breasts rubbing his back? Coming while they drove was not an option. They'd stop for coffee, that's all. He'd take care of business in the bathroom. Yeah. They'd stop for coffee. Often.

Maybe he could grab a cup right now.

"Where's your motorcycle?" she asked.

"Come on, I'll show you."

He took her hand and led her out the side door to the lot where he kept most of the bikes. She seemed pretty impressed. Wait'll she got a load of his baby.

Walking her the few shorts steps to his parking space, he watched for her reaction. The ladies always went nuts over his bike. Knowing Amelia's fantasy about being ravished by a biker made the moment all the sweeter. "There she is," he said, then he stepped back.

She stared at the bike for a moment, then gave him a crooked little smile. "It's pretty."

His balloon burst with a *pop*. "Pretty?"

She nodded. "Oh, yeah. I think it's the prettiest one here."

"Pretty?"

"I'm sorry. Did I say something wrong?"

"No. No, not at all. You're right. It is pretty." He shoved the key into the ignition. "You ready?"

"Wait a minute. What's wrong?"

"Nothing."

She crossed her arms. "Please tell me. I'll be so worried about it, I won't have a good time."

He looked up at the sky, at the billowing clouds. So what if she said his bike was "pretty"? It didn't matter. It was just a word. It didn't change the bike, make it any less his pride and joy. Dammit, this was all going exactly the way he'd wanted it to, so why would he want to screw it up because of one word? He turned to her.

"It's nothing. It's stupid. I just don't think of my bike as pretty, that's all."

"Oh. I meant that as a compliment. It's a very impressive motorcycle. Really."

He waved a dismissive hand. "Come on, forget about it. Let's get this show on the road."

She nodded, but he could tell she felt bad. He mounted the bike, then patted the seat behind him. "It's okay, babe."

She took in a deep breath—which did incredible things to the sweater—and climbed onto the leather seat. Her thighs pressed against his hips in a way that made him forget his wounded ego. When her arms went around his waist, he had to hold back a groan. Impatiently, he waited to feel her chest against his back. It didn't happen. She wasn't holding him tightly enough. He took her hands in his and pulled her forward. When there was no room between them, he let her go. "Ready?"

"I've never done this before."

He grinned. "I have a feeling there are going to be a lot of firsts between us." Then he turned the key, revved the powerful engine, and they roared out of there as pretty as you please.

IT WAS SENSORY OVERLOAD. The vibration of the bike between her legs, the way her thighs spread to accommodate his hips, her breasts pressed tight against him, her hands touching his hard body—she didn't know what to concentrate on first.

Simply the fact that it was *her* made her head spin. Shy, invisible Amelia, on the back of a Harley-Davidson with the most gorgeous guy in the universe—it was beyond comprehension. There were none of the qualities of a dream, and she didn't think she'd gone completely delusional. If she had, she didn't care. This was good. This was the best thing that had happened to her in—ever.

She wanted to rest her head on his shoulder, but she couldn't quite get up the nerve. Touching him this way was already so intimate. Of course, he had kissed her. Twice. But she still wasn't ready to take another step. Not yet. She'd done enough for one day. The jeans belonged to Donna, the sweater to Kathy; the makeup was Tabby's; and she'd gone, first thing this morning, to Victoria's Secret and splurged on a matching pair of pink lace panties and bra.

Not that he was going to see it, but it made her feel sexy. Pretty. She wasn't used to feeling pretty. Her aunt Grace, as loving as she'd been, had made it very clear that vanity was a sin, and that showing off would only get Amelia into trouble. She'd learned that lesson herself years later. She'd grown so comfortable in her invisibility that even wearing jeans and a sweater seemed unbearably daring.

She'd never guessed riding a motorcycle could be so erotic. It was like a giant B.O.B.—battery-operated boyfriend. At least, that's what Kathy called hers. If more women took rides on these babies, they'd never settle for a car again.

They slipped through traffic, passing stalled cars, honking taxi drivers, limos and buses. While it thrilled her, it was also somewhat scary, and at Lexington, she decided to close her eyes. Which wasn't such a great plan. She grabbed hold of Jay's shirt…well, actually, more than his shirt. He jerked, the bike swerved.

"I'm sorry," she said, but she had no idea if he heard her. But then, without giving herself time to think or pause, she pulled his T-shirt up, releasing it from his jeans. She took a deep breath, then touched his naked chest.

The bike swerved again, and she couldn't help it, she scratched him. Not deeply, but the whole idea of her nails on his skin took her breath away. With shocking boldness, she continued to touch him.

She'd had this fantasy for a long time about sex with a biker. They'd ride off into a secluded wood, and then he'd turn around and he'd unzip his pants, showing her just how hot and hard he was. She'd be so excited that she'd sit right down on his lap, and instead of riding the bike, she'd ride him.

Almost swooning with the image, she let herself explore. With the scent of leather and the roar of the traffic all around, her fingers moved slowly over his skin, learning, memorizing, so that when this was all over, her fantasies would be incredibly detailed.

There was so little padding on him. Just taut flesh over muscle. Not like her at all, and certainly not like Kevin. He'd been nice and all, but he'd also been shaped like a pear. Jay, on the other hand, had the body of an Adonis. Okay, so that was a bit much, but damn, he was fine. Just enough hair on his chest. Oh. Really hard little nipples. She could feel his tension, and she wondered if it was caused by driving, or by her leisurely study. Maybe she should lay off. With the traffic this heavy, it was dangerous, and she wasn't through with him yet.

She smiled at the bold thought. As if she'd ever say or do anything remotely like that. Truth was, she was all hat and no cowboy. But that was changing, wasn't it? Starting with a pair of snug jeans and some lipstick, and her own fierce determination.

Her fantasy man had walked into her life, and she wasn't about to let him go. She had a lot to make up for—years and years of hiding, running, feeling less-than. If she didn't go for it now, she was afraid she never would.

He swerved again, and she gripped him tighter, and then they were at the curb. With the engine idling, he turned to face her, and she quickly slipped her hands from under his shirt. He gave her the oddest smile. "There's something I have to do before we leave the city."

Something about him had changed, and she couldn't read his expression. Now her pulse raced with a different kind of energy. It was her brazenness. He was shocked. Well, so was she. The question, however, was if he was pleased or put off.

Before she could ask, he turned and guided the bike back into traffic. This time, she held his waist over his shirt. And she didn't lay her cheek on his leather jacket. She just wondered what had gotten into her.

For all intents and purposes, Jay was a stranger. She'd only talked to him a couple of times. He could be anything, anyone, and she'd given herself to him without question. She didn't know where they were headed, or what they'd do when they got there. And while all that was scary, it was also more exciting than anything she could remember. Her grip tightened.

After two more long blocks, Jay turned right, then slowed. He drove up next to an old brownstone and cut the engine. She didn't recognize the neighborhood, and the only people she saw on the street were an elderly couple holding grocery bags and a man walking a Doberman.

She got off the motorcycle, and Jay did, too. After they took off their helmets, she got a better look at his face. He seemed angry, his brow furrowed and his lips pressed tightly together.

Her hand went to her neck. His gaze focused there for a moment, then he looked into her eyes.

"Come on. Let's get this done."

She swallowed. He couldn't mean... "Jay, where are we?"

He looked at her crookedly, as if surprised by the question. "My apartment."

Uh-oh.

7

JAY COULDN'T BELIEVE he'd forgotten his promise. Of all the rotten timing. He took Amelia's hand and led her to the building's big glass doors. She hesitated a moment as they passed the threshold, and when he glanced at her expression, he stopped short.

"What's wrong?"

She tried to smile at him, but she didn't quite pull it off. "Nothing."

"Nope. I'm not buying it."

She looked up. At first he thought she was praying or something, and then he got it.

"It's okay," he said, fighting not to laugh. "You're safe."

Then he did laugh when he saw the flash of disappointment cross her face.

"It's not funny," she said, but she was grinning, too.

"Wait'll you get a load of our chaperones." He didn't want to explain further. Let her see for herself.

They stepped in the elevator, her hand still in his. He wanted to get on with it, to get her out of the city, out of her comfort zone. Who was he kidding? He wanted to stop the elevator and ravish her right now, but he didn't want to have to look for a new apartment.

"What?"

"Hmm?"

"You were looking at me funny." She stepped a little closer to him, studying him as if his face held clues.

"I was just wishing we didn't have to do this. But I promised."

"And you're not going to tell me what this is, right?"

He shook his head. The elevator climbed slowly up to his floor, and the doors opened. He remembered the last woman he'd brought to his place. She was a six-foot beauty who was into leather and acrobatics. They'd stayed in for three days. He'd like to do the same with Amelia, but that wasn't going to happen. Not today, anyway. She wanted to ride. He'd take her. It was her fantasy, and she deserved to have it come true. It didn't hurt that he was getting what he wanted at the same time. Symmetry. That's what it was. Perfect symmetry.

They went down the hall, past his place to Shawn and Bill's apartment. He had to knock loudly, because neither one of the old men could hear worth a damn.

Amelia continued to watch him in her quiet way. What was she thinking? She wasn't easy to read. Which made the game that much more fun.

He went to bang on the door again, but it opened, and he caught himself in mid-swing. Bill's eyes widened as he saw what could have been a TKO.

"All right, all right," he said. "I'll call a plumber."

Jay laughed. The old guys might be deaf and they were mostly a pain in the ass, but they cracked him up. "Bill, I'd like you to meet Amelia."

Bill shifted his gaze, and smiled so wide that Jay could see his bridgework. "Amelia? Nice to meet you." He stepped back, opening the door wider. "Come in, come in. Don't mind the smell. Shawn is making corned beef and cabbage. Not that I can eat it, mind you. My stomach would be upset for days, and then he'd complain about the smell, all right."

"Hey, Bill," Jay said, knowing what he was about to say would make no difference at all. "You know the concept of too much information?"

Bill waved his hand as if he were swatting flies. "We're friends. Friends can say anything."

Amelia smiled at him, and it was all over for the old man. He was smitten. Jay didn't blame him. It was pretty hard not to be attracted to her, now that she wasn't hiding.

"So, you and Jay…?" Bill wiggled his eyebrows.

Amelia blushed, and Jay's cock responded. When her cheeks got pink like that, it did something to him.

"We're, uh, friends," she said. Then she looked at him as if for confirmation. Or contradiction.

"Soon to be much more," he said, keeping his voice so low that he knew Bill wouldn't be able to hear. Amelia, however, didn't know Bill was mostly deaf, and her blush went from pink to crimson.

Bill squinted at him. "What?"

"Do you want your sink fixed, or not?"

Sighing heavily, Bill shook his head as he led them to the kitchen.

Jay still had Amelia's hand in his, and he gave it a squeeze when they came upon Shawn at the stove. The old man wore an apron with Kiss the Cook emblazoned on the front.

"Look who Jay brought," Bill said. "Her name is Amelia."

Shawn gave her the once-over, then nodded. "Nice. In fact, very nice." He scowled at Jay. "This is the kind of girl you should be dating."

"Yeah, yeah." Jay touched Amelia's cheek. "Ignore them."

"I don't think I should."

"Trust me. They're both lunatics."

"I heard that," Shawn said. He put his hands on his hips. "Just because we're willing to tell the truth…"

Jay kissed Amelia lightly on the lips. "We'll be outta here in five." He went to the sink, opened the cabinet below it and took out the wrench, then got down on the floor. The plumbing sucked in the building, but Shawn's apartment had it the worst. Jay cleared the sink at least a couple of times a month. The super had promised to fix it. Right.

He laid down on his back and maneuvered under the pipes until he could get the wrench in place. Luckily, it would only take a few minutes to fix. Because if he had to wait much longer to feel Amelia's hands under his shirt again, he'd lose it.

He could just see her legs from here. They shouldn't have made his pulse race, but they did. Just seeing her legs, for God's sake, and in jeans, no less. He needed help, and he'd get right on it. Tomorrow. Today, he needed to fix the friggin' pipes.

"Amelia," Shawn said. "That's a lovely name for a lovely girl."

"Thank you."

"What do you do, sweetheart?"

"I'm in grad school."

"What are you—"

The pot on the stove must have bubbled over, because Shawn's curses were accompanied by sizzling. Jay concentrated on the pipes, loosened a nut, then realized he hadn't brought the bucket.

"Amelia?"

She bent down so he could see her face. Damn. He had to work faster.

"Would you bring me the bucket? Shawn will give it to you."

She walked away, and he changed his mind about where he was going to take her. He'd thought about Long Island—Port Washington, to be exact. Right on the ocean, it was a beautiful town with great restaurants. But it was also crowded. He knew a place upstate that would afford them a lot more privacy. A little bed-and-breakfast in Woodstock where he'd spent a weekend maybe a year ago. Yeah. Much better.

"Here."

She bent down again, holding up the bucket. He

couldn't take it until he moved to his right. He swapped her for the wrench, and positioned the bucket under the pipe. The nut sufficiently loosened, he unscrewed it the rest of the way, and in short order, he'd cleared the clog. Craning his neck, he could only see her legs.

"You have that wrench?"

"Uh-huh."

She leaned over, but before he could reach out for the tool, it slipped from her hand and landed right on his nuts. The pain rocked him forward. He slammed his forehead into the pipe and dropped the bucket of sludge on his legs.

"Oh God." Amelia crouched down beside him. "I'm so sorry."

He couldn't make her feel better at the moment. Not while he was incapacitated. It didn't help matters to hear Shawn and Bill laughing like hyenas. Why'd it have to fall *there?* Another wave of pain washed through him, and he prayed he wouldn't be sick.

"Jay? Are you okay? Oh God. I can't believe I did that."

"It's okay," he mumbled through clenched teeth. He picked up the wrench from the floor and handed the bucket to Amelia.

She took it, but she kept staring at him. Her concern would have been touching if he hadn't wanted to curl up in a little ball and weep.

She stood, and he used all his willpower to finish the job under the sink. Despite his soaked jeans, which, he had just discovered, smelled like week-old fish. When the pipe was snug, he crawled out and sat up. He wasn't ready to stand, yet.

Amelia crouched down next to him. "Ow, ow, ow." She touched the goose egg on his forehead.

"Ah."

Drawing in a sharp breath between her teeth, she backed off. "Sorry. I'm sorry."

He nodded, grateful that the pain in his head was now greater than the pain in his crotch.

Amelia stood up and went to the freezer. Shawn gave her a towel, and she wrapped up a handful of ice. Then she was back, next to him, and she put the towel on his bruise.

"Ow."

"I'm sorry."

"You don't have to be sorry."

"But it's my fault."

"It was an accident." He moved, not able to hold back a grimace.

Amelia shook her head, her beautiful face a mask of concern. Then she took the wrapped ice and put it in his lap. Hard.

He winced. She jerked back. Shawn and Bill laughed their asses off.

"Don't put the ice there," Bill said. "You know what happens."

She turned to him. "What?"

Bill laughed louder, slapping the counter with his hand. "Shrinkage. And if you're going to do what I think you're going to do, he needs his equipment in working order."

Amelia's blush actually made him feel better. Not great. But better.

"Hey," he whispered. "Come here."

Still looking stricken, she sat down next to him. He wanted her to scoot closer so he could put his arm around her, but in his current state, that wasn't going to happen. She'd get soaked, and then they'd both smell like dead carp.

"I'm sorry."

"No more apologies. I'm fine."

Out of the corner of his eye, he saw Shawn drag Bill out of the room. A small miracle.

"You're not fine. I nearly crippled you."

He touched her chin with his index finger. "I can assure you, there's no permanent damage."

Her expression relaxed, and a slight smile curved her pink lips. "We shouldn't go."

"Why not?" he asked. He shifted and winced at the pain in his groin, which answered his own question. Two hours on a bike? With her? Yeah, he'd be crippled.

"That's why."

He nodded. "Another day."

She took his hand in hers and brought his palm to her lips, giving him the most delicate of kisses. That started a chain reaction that he couldn't have stopped for anything. He moved his hand and kissed her. Gently, soothingly. At least, at first. But when he felt her warm tongue touch his bottom lip, he cried uncle. He opened his mouth, and they teased each other with darting, swirling tongues. He groaned when she nipped his lip, and when he thrust inside her sweet mouth, she whimpered.

Some small part of his brain registered that he was, indeed, completely functional, although there was a distinctive throb of a completely different kind that, while it didn't exactly hurt, didn't feel great, either. But dammit, he wanted her. Now. Right now. On the floor in his neighbors' apartment. His fingers slipped through the soft silk of her hair, then lingered on her shoulder. She shuddered as he deepened the kiss and ran his hand down her chest until he touched the top of her swelling breast.

Her breath hitched, and he froze, but when she sucked the tip of his tongue, he nearly lost it. Cupping her breast, he felt how hard her nipple was, even through the sweater and her bra. Like his cock, she was at attention, in full-need mode. He gently squeezed her flesh, eliciting another moan.

"All right, you two," Shawn said from somewhere. "Get a room. I've got corned beef to cook."

She bit down, and Jay cried out, sure his tongue was toast. Amelia jerked away.

"It's only me," Shawn said, heading to the stove. "No need to be embarrassed."

"I'm sorry," she said to Jay. "I can't believe this."

Jay touched his tongue with his finger. No blood. The pain had eased considerably, enough for him to ignore it and tend to Amelia. "It's okay."

"It's not."

He couldn't help his grin. "Honey, you're going to have to get up," he whispered as gently as he could.

"I know," she said, although she didn't move.

Shawn shook his wooden spoon in the general direction of the sink. "Don't be ridiculous. Amelia, I need to ask some questions. He'll be fine. He's been bitten in worse places, I'm sure."

Jay gave him a scathing look, as if that would shut the old coot up.

"So, darling," Shawn said, ignoring Jay completely. "Tell me something. You cook?"

It worked. She started to relax. She nodded.

"Any specialties?"

She blinked a couple of times. "Um, I don't... Well, I make a good lasagna."

Shawn nodded, and Jay's suspicion mounted. What was his neighbor up to?

"You like to read?"

"Very much."

"Good. Because he's a reader. And a writer. Why don't you ask him about it when you leave?"

Jay scrabbled to his feet, ignoring the pain, ready to tell Shawn to mind his own business. But then he felt Amelia's hand on his leg, and Shawn was saved. Damn busybody.

Amelia frowned, and Jay smiled, not wanting her to think his ire was directed at her.

She turned to Shawn. "We should go now."

Shawn came over and kissed her on the forehead. "Be safe. Be kind."

"Can I ask you a question?"

"Yes."

"I understand, I think, about wanting to know if I like to read. But why did you want to know if I can cook?"

"Because I like to eat. And Jay can't cook worth shit."

She laughed out loud. Jay just watched her. She changed when she laughed. Lightened up in a way that made her shine. It was her laugh that told him most about her secret self. Uninhibited and sweet... Like a diamond, there were a hundred facets to this shy girl from the cyber café. And he wanted to explore each and every one.

AMELIA WAVED as Bill shut the door. "They're nice."

Jay nodded. "They were good friends with my grandfather."

"Were?"

He took her hand to lead her back to the elevator, but he slowed as he neared his apartment. "He died a few months ago. This used to be his place."

"Were you two close?"

"Yeah. Real close. He was...great. You'd have liked him."

Amelia caught the change in his voice, although his expression didn't alter a bit. He was a man used to hiding his feelings. He accused her of being the invisible one—but wasn't this almost the same? While she was cloaked in baggy sweaters and skirts, he hid behind his leather jacket and his charisma. His tough-guy image.

He loved his grandfather. He helped his elderly neighbors. She'd never have guessed, but it pleased her a great deal. She'd been prepared for him to be a self-serving bastard. A man that good-looking was usually arrogant beyond measure. Maybe Jay had arrogant moments, but his actions were generous. Shawn had made it a point to say he was a writer. Jay's reaction intrigued her. She'd explore that later. If there was going to be a later.

Whether there was a future for them or not, she'd like to read whatever he wrote. It would be good, of that she had no doubt. His manner was educated, sophisticated and intense. A great combination.

"Come on," he said as he tugged her hand. "I've got to get out of these clothes."

SOME PEOPLE DIDN'T BELIEVE in fate. They were fools. Because what else could have brought Amelia to his apartment, where she'd gone immediately to the bookcase, which put her in a direct line with the mirror in his bedroom…where he was about to get naked. Oh, and he couldn't leave out the part about how his having to get naked was her fault.

It was worth a wrench on the balls. And he couldn't think of one other damn thing he could say that about.

She scanned his shelves avidly, and he tried to remember where he'd put his novel. Under something, he thought, so he should be safe. Or maybe, if she did find it, that would be the reason she'd turn toward the bedroom. Look down the hall. Into the mirror.

He positioned himself so that she would only see his reflection, not his body. He could see her, too, but he had to be careful not to be caught staring, or she'd know it wasn't an accident.

He kicked off his boots, threw his jacket on the bed. Then he unbuttoned his shirt, getting rid of it as quickly as possible. She might look this way any second, and he needed to be ready.

Once he got to his belt, he paused. In her fantasy, the guy was already naked when she looked. But maybe it would be even sexier if he was in the midst of stripping.

Screw it. She'd already written the script. All he had to do was play his part. He unbuttoned his jeans and slipped them off, taking his boxers at the same time.

There. He was naked. And Little Jay was damn happy about it. He checked the mirror. Shit. Where was she—? Okay. She hadn't run out the door screaming. She still had her attention focused on the books.

What if she didn't turn? How long was he supposed to stand here? His legs were still damp—

He cursed silently as he dashed into his bathroom. How sexy would it have been for her to come down the hall, sink to her knees, and turn green because he smelled like garbage? Fate might be in charge, but the details were still in his backyard.

He washed quickly, dried more quickly still, and

made it back into position without breaking a sweat. However, his penis had gone flaccid, and that wasn't right.

Not that it was so bad to look at, but the script said hard, and he wanted to be hard. He glanced at her reflection. She had found a book to look at on the top shelf. Her sweater had ridden up as she reached for it, showing off her delectable ass.

Well, that took care of his problem. Now, all he had to do was get her to look. He wanted her to do it spontaneously. He willed her to look, focused on it with all his might.

After a few moments, his gaze went to his reflection instead of hers, and he turned a little to the right. Sucked in his gut. Ran a hand through his hair. Then froze as he realized what it would look like if she saw him now.

He closed his eyes, cursing himself for being such a jackass. He shifted, not even sure where to stand, what to do. He hadn't thought this part through. If she caught him looking at her reflection, it was all over. She'd think he was a pervert, and she'd be out of here in two seconds flat. He'd be lucky if she didn't call the police. So if he couldn't look at her, how would he know she was looking at him?

His impromptu plan fell around him in an undignified heap. It was time to end the game, call it a forfeit and figure out what he was going to do with Ms. Amelia once he was dressed.

Only, the decision got put on hold when he looked up to see a pair of very startled green eyes staring at him in the mirror.

8

AMELIA FROZE. Naked. He was naked. Completely naked, and she could see his— Oh God. As she stared, utterly unable to move a muscle, he grew. It was like watching a wind sock fill with air.

She should go. Now. Right now.

Her gaze moved back up to his eyes. Chocolate-brown eyes. Finely drawn, sharp features... The straight line of the shoulders, the unconsciously graceful way he held himself. Well-muscled arms, the beautifully molded, smooth chest marred only by a thin scar by his right shoulder. Slim hips and flat stomach. A line of dark hair beginning low on his abdomen, widening to where the erection stood away from his body.

The man was a work of art. Golden skin and rippling muscle. Controlled power and fierce male beauty.

And he was real. Not a fantasy. Or perhaps he was the ultimate fantasy. She wasn't sure anymore. It didn't matter. All she had to do was walk into his room. Touch him. Get down on her knees...

She took a step.

His lips parted and his chest rose as he inhaled deeply.

She took another step, her gaze moving from his eyes, to his chest, to his dark, thick—

Oh God. What was she doing? She practically threw herself at the door. Her hand fumbled on the knob as he called her name. She couldn't stay another second. She could never look at him again.

The door opened and she bolted, making it to the elevator in two seconds and pounding on the button.

"Amelia."

She looked back. He stood in his doorway, his shirt held over his crotch. His chest heaving with deep draughts of air, his gaze troubled.

Of course his gaze was troubled. She'd just caught him naked. Yes, they'd kissed, but...oh God.

"Amelia, don't go. I'm sorry."

Where was the stupid elevator? She punched the button again. "I'm the one who's sorry," she said, staring at the elevator doors. "I didn't know. I would never have looked."

Her face was about to burst into flames. She couldn't believe it. First she clobbered his penis, then this. And she'd almost walked right up to him.

A hand on her shoulder stopped her cold.

"Amelia. Wait."

She glanced at him. Still naked. Just the shirt covering his front. In the hallway. She moaned and covered her face with her hands.

"Come back inside. I'll get dressed. It's no big deal."

She peeked through her fingers. "No big deal? I'd die."

He smiled. "I didn't."

She squeezed her eyes shut. "I'm being a dope, aren't I."

"No. You're not."

"Yes, I am. I'm twenty-four. I shouldn't be hysterical over seeing a man naked."

"I caught you off guard, that's all."

She brought her hands down. Opened her eyes to his gaze. He looked so concerned. She sighed. "I'm sorry. I've botched up everything."

"You haven't. Come back. We'll have coffee."

She shook her head. "I can't."

"Why not?"

How could she explain? First, to see him stark naked, then to overreact like a child. She'd screwed up royally. "I have to go."

He squeezed her shoulder. "Come on back. I'll put on some pants. You'll see. Everything will be fine."

"I'd think you'd be running for your life. With all I've done today—"

He laughed. "Hey, at least we got that awkward getting naked stage half over with."

Her lips curled up despite herself. "You're joking. Standing in the hallway butt naked, and you're trying to put me at ease."

"Everyone on this floor has seen an ass before, I assure you."

She giggled. "I bet they haven't seen that ass."

"I don't think so. But there was that one New Year's Eve…"

Her shoulders relaxed, and the heat in her face had cooled considerably. "I really should go. I have to study, and I work tomorrow."

He looked at her for a moment. "Where?"

"The university library."

His responding "of course" smile made her wince.

"Okay, you can go. But only because you have to study."

The elevator arrived with a *ding*. She looked at the doors as they opened, then turned back to Jay. "Thanks. For a very interesting day."

He grinned.

"Next time, maybe we should just go to a movie or something."

His eyes grew serious. "There will be a next time. You do know that, right?"

She nodded. "I promised a week."

"Good." He pulled her close and kissed her gently on the lips. Her breasts brushed his chest and she gasped.

"Oh, Amelia. You are one of a kind."

"That's one way of putting it." She stepped into the elevator, but put her hand on the open button. "Goodbye."

"Study hard."

She nodded.

He turned and headed for his door. Her gaze went straight down to his butt.

She clamped her mouth shut before she moaned. It

was perfect. The most gorgeous rear view in history. Long legs elegantly muscled, firm buttocks perfectly shaped, athletic back and shoulders, soft dark hair falling over the nape of his neck...

She whimpered as she released the elevator button. His laughter slipped in just before the doors shut.

JAY LEANED BACK in his chair, his feet up on his desk, the keyboard on his lap. He'd just logged on to TrueConfessions.com and was scrolling through the later entries of Good Girl.

It had been two days since he'd seen her. Two days of thinking about her, running the tape in his mind over and over—the one where she sees him and she stares and her eyes get huge and hot, and her lips part ever so slightly, and she takes a step as if she has no control over herself—

He cuts the tape before she runs out of his apartment.

It wasn't a mistake. It was a learning experience. Now he knew more about Amelia. About the difference between her fantasies and her reality. And he'd make adjustments.

He'd leave soon. She was at the café. Brian had called, and now expected a brake job on his bike. It was a fair trade. Brian said she was wearing jeans but she was back to the cardigan. And her hair was up. Forward three steps, back two.

So it would be different this time. More cerebral. But still, he wasn't about to let her off the hook. The woman part of her needed attention so badly it scared the hell out of her. He could see it in her eyes, on the page, in the way she touched the back of her neck.

She needed to feel comfortable. To trust him. That's what he'd focus on. Trust. Different kinds of trust.

He got to an entry he hadn't read before. Written yesterday. He put the keyboard down, dragged his feet off the desk and leaned close to the monitor.

He kissed me. It was the best moment. The most fully alive moment. He scares me to death, and draws me to him in a way that's inescapable. I think of Dracula. The novel, not the movies. That sexual force he had that took all power, all freedom of choice from his victims. An outsider would say they walked into his arms willingly, yearning for his deadly touch. But the helplessness came before the first step. The spell was cast through the air or through the soul or maybe it was just that his need for them was so great, they simply had no choice.

I want to make a choice. I want to see J for who he is, and not who I want him to be. But I don't know, maybe it's already too late.

He reads me like a book. He touches the deepest parts of me, and he makes me crazy stupid when I'm near him.

He hasn't called, but I know he'll call. It's only been a day. He'll call tomorrow.

Jay read it twice. It was a lot to think about. He wondered, of the two of them, who cast the spell. It was nuts, how he'd focused on this one woman. He'd worked, talked on the phone, done some stuff with his portfolio, just like normal life—only it wasn't.

She was there all the time. Even at his busiest, she hovered on the periphery, never truly out of sight. During the calm, she bloomed in his mind, took over his thoughts, his senses.

The key here was to play it out. It wasn't her so much as The Plan. The end result. He had to see her when she let it all go. All the inhibitions, all the rules and regulations. It would be like that one step. Like her lips parting.

He scrolled down. Another entry, made the same day.

I dreamed I kept walking. He was naked, and I kept walking, and it was the embodiment of my most secret desires. How did that happen? I didn't realize until I read it again, but what occurred at J's apartment was almost exactly what I'd written a year ago. Before I'd met him.

It's scary. And wonderful. It makes me want to see what comes next. I wonder if I should call. I don't know. I've had so little experience with men. I don't mind so much, except that it undermines my confidence, which is shaky to begin with. My time with J didn't bolster me much. Well, part of it did. The part where he looked at me as if he wanted to climb inside me. And the kiss.

In my dream, he kissed me, and I was dressed while he was naked, and I got to touch him wherever I wanted to. His chest, his nipples, the indent on the side of his behind. I got to take his hard length in my hand, and in my mouth. He offered himself to me, and I took it. Selfishly. Disregarding his modesty, his needs.

It was wonderful.

This doesn't feel like my life.

Jay knew exactly what she meant. It wasn't his life, either. It was better.

He logged off, put his empty coffee cup in the sink, grabbed his jacket and headed out.

9

AMELIA LOOKED UP the moment Jay walked in the door. As always, so did every other customer in the café. She blushed, naturally, and looked down, but only for a moment. She had to see if he searched her out, if he smiled when he saw her. If the hunger was still there.

Her gaze moved up his black jeans, pausing at his fly. No, it was her imagination. Even if there was a bulge, it didn't mean anything. He wore a gray shirt, something slinky and retro under his ever-present leather jacket. Nice. Very nice. Finally, she dared to look at his face. His lips curved into a sexy grin and he didn't notice anyone else, and the hunger was there, alive in his eyes. With every step, her awareness heightened, and nervous excitement coursed through her body, settling in the juncture of her thighs.

She knew his body, now. She'd seen his chest, his hips. She'd seen it all, and it was stunning. But the knowledge changed things. The stakes had been raised. It wasn't theoretical any longer. She couldn't deny that he wanted her. Which made her desire for him nearly unbearable.

He reached her table, pulled a chair from the work-station next to hers and straddled it. So close his knee touched her leg, sending heat to all the important places.

"Hey, gorgeous."

Her blush deepened. "Hi."

"Studying?"

She nodded. "I've got a term paper due soon."

"Pity."

"Why?"

"Because I want to take you away."

Her heart fluttered. "You do?"

He nodded. His grin had gone, but there was still that look in his eyes that said he wanted to do much more than take her away.

"Where?"

"You'll find out."

"But I have to study."

"Okay."

She frowned. Such arrogance to sit there so smugly. She should tell him to leave, just so he'd know she wasn't putty in his hands. Even if she was.

Her hand went to the mouse almost of its own accord, and she saved her work, made a backup on a floppy disk. When she turned to him again, he was standing, holding out his hand.

She placed her palm in the warm cradle, let him help her up. He didn't let go when she stood next to him. His nearness made it hard to breathe, and she felt light-headed, dizzy with his scent, a mixture of soap and musk, and with his heat. His warm breath caressed her cheek, and she turned to face him squarely.

She didn't realize she'd been praying for his kiss until his lips touched hers. Then all she could think of was "Thank you."

He pulled back after a quick flick of his tongue on her lower lip. "Come on," he whispered in a voice like black velvet.

Her bag in her free hand, she followed him from the café, vaguely wondering if she'd remembered to log out.

His bike was at the curb. He handed her a helmet, then frowned.

"What?"

"You don't have a jacket?"

"I was going home after I finished working."

"How far away is your place?"

"About four blocks."

He put on his helmet, climbed on the bike, and waited for her to do the same. She hesitated, and he cocked his head to the right.

She was chilly already. It would be stupid to freeze just so Jay wouldn't meet her roommates. She gave him her address, but she had a bad feeling she'd just made a terrible mistake.

IT WAS NONDESCRIPT in the way so many New York buildings were. Six stories, no doorman. That wasn't so good. Jay parked the bike and, after he pocketed his keys, headed toward the door. But Amelia hesitated.

"What's wrong?"

"Nothing." She gave him a brave grin, which proved that she'd just lied, then led him inside. Her elevator worked quickly, and it smelled like lemons, which was a big improvement over wet dog. They stopped on the third floor, the second door on the right.

After fumbling with the three locks, she finally got the door open, and music hit him square in the chest. Loud music. Creed. So she didn't live alone.

"Come on in," she said, grimacing at the pounding beat. "My roommates like testing the sound barrier."

"I can tell."

"One minute." She had to yell over the throbbing bass. With a determined pull to her lips, she headed toward the back of the flat and disappeared behind a door.

Jay looked around. The apartment wasn't bad, as far as Manhattan apartments went. There was an actual living room and kitchen. Some students he'd known lived in shoe boxes, with bathtubs in the kitchen. This place was downright roomy.

He could see Amelia's touch. Not in the scattered high heels by the couch, or the newspaper spread on the floor, but in the curtains—white with blue stripes, tied with a satin ribbon. Her mark was on the flower arrangement resting on the mantel, and the candles by the wing chair.

"Hello."

He turned toward the low, feminine voice. A blonde smiled at him from the hallway.

"And who might you be?"

"Jay."

Her smile showed off even white teeth and an invitation. "I'm Donna."

"Hi."

She walked toward him, moving like she knew how to use her body. Her sweater was just small enough to show every damn curve, but just big enough to keep her from an indecent exposure charge. She'd poured herself into her jeans. Oh, yeah. She knew what she was doing.

"Did you come here with someone? Or is this destiny?"

The music stopped so suddenly it hurt. The silence pulsed for a few seconds, and then Amelia came back, wearing a dark blue sweater over her jeans. A brunette in leggings and a sweatshirt followed close on her heels.

"Hey, Donna, who's your friend?"

"He doesn't belong to me," the blonde said, "which is such a shame."

"I'm Kathy," the woman in leggings said, holding out her hand. Her nails were long, painted a dark red.

He shook her hand. "Jay."

"So, how did you meet Tabby?"

He looked at Amelia, then back at Kathy. "Tabby?"

"You're not with…?"

He walked over to Amelia, and slipped his arm around her waist. "You ready, babe?"

The looks she got from her roommates told him a

hell of a lot. They didn't know anything about Amelia, either of them. He doubted very much they had even tried to know her.

She smiled up at him. "Let me get my coat." She disappeared down that same hallway.

"You're with Amelia?" Donna asked.

"Yeah, I am. Why?"

"Well, I just…" Donna looked imploringly at Kathy.

"She doesn't date much."

"Lucky me."

Kathy studied him, clearly perplexed. "Where did you meet her?"

He didn't care for these girls. And they were "girls," no matter their age. "I met her in a café."

Kathy came closer. "So, you've known her a while?"

"Long enough."

Donna approached him from the other side. "Is it the jeans? Those are my jeans, you know."

He arched his brow. "It's not the jeans."

"Wow."

"Yeah. Wow—"

A flash of movement caught his eye, and he turned to see Amelia, jacket in hand, standing in the hallway. He wondered how much she'd heard. And if she believed him. It had to be murder living with these two. He crossed the room, took her coat and slipped it on her. Then he put his arm around her waist to walk her out.

Kathy turned toward Amelia. "You go, girl."

Amelia blushed but she didn't hesitate.

Jay nodded at Donna as they passed, and he had to chuckle at her confusion.

He walked Amelia to the door, but just this side of the threshold he kissed her, and he didn't stop until he was damn good and ready. He grinned at the sighs coming from the roommates, as he and Amelia walked into the hallway.

THE DREAM CONTINUED as Jay led her back down to his bike. He touched her in a way that changed everything. It was as if her senses had been dull all these years, and whenever he took her hand, or stroked the small of her back, she saw with new eyes. Colors had become more vivid, scents more evocative. On some level, she knew it was a chemical response, but mostly it just felt like magic.

She still couldn't get over her roommates' reaction to Jay, although she wasn't unreservedly pleased. She understood why they couldn't picture her with someone like Jay, because *she* couldn't picture it. That's what made her a little sad. That she'd been so sure no one wonderful could want her.

Her self-esteem needed some work, and so far, Jay was what the doctor ordered. Even as they began their trip, she marveled at the way he made sure her helmet was on correctly, that she was warm, that she held him tightly enough as they zoomed into the street.

Talk about exhilaration. The wind, the deft maneuvering of the bike, the feel of her breasts pressing into his leather jacket, the vibration between her legs…sensory overload of the most incredible kind.

She wondered where he would take her. Someplace quiet. Private. A hotel? A secret hideaway? And once they got there, what then? He'd told her straight out that he wanted to make love with her, and although it scared her, she couldn't deny her own need.

But they hardly knew each other. Her old-fashioned notions didn't include sex on a second date. Not even the tenth date. According to her aunt, she shouldn't even think of such things until the wedding. She'd removed that option several years ago, although she and Kevin had known each other quite a while before they'd gone to bed. Of course, that had ended in abject failure.

That was what made this adventure with Jay so frightening. After all this time, she still wondered what she'd done wrong that night. How she could have been so unexciting that Kevin had actually fallen asleep!

If she didn't know how she'd screwed up, it seemed inevitable that she'd do it again. The thought of Jay falling asleep in the middle of making love made her shudder.

He turned a sharp corner and her hands tightened around his waist. Such an incredibly buff body. She knew that firsthand. She'd never been this intimate with a man so solid and sculpted. He was like someone from the movies, or at the very least a Calvin Klein billboard.

They headed uptown, the traffic on the crisp, cool

afternoon unusually heavy. She didn't care where they were going or how fast they got there, because she was already there. This was the place she'd dreamed about. Touching him. Being close to him.

Only, she could feel the tension in him. His muscles tightened, his chest rose and fell more rapidly. He dodged and darted between cabs and limos and city buses, but no matter how he tried, he couldn't escape the crush of cars.

As if the traffic wasn't bad enough, a sprinkling of raindrops splashed on her visor.

They slowed for a stoplight, and she leaned close to his ear. "Jay, we don't have to do this today."

He turned his head. "What?"

"Whatever it is you planned. We can do it another time."

He frowned. "I wanted to take you away."

She touched his lips with her fingertips. "You already have."

He kissed her fingers, and his smile shifted her reality again, turning everything that wasn't Jay into a bland gray mush.

"Hang on," he said, as he turned the bike around. She refused to speculate on where they were going, what they would do. She didn't want to focus on later. Right now was perfect.

10

HE PARKED THE BIKE in a small space between a Hummer stretch limo and a tan Volvo. Amelia didn't move, even when he cut the engine. He turned his head to look at her, not surprised to see her eyes wide, staring up at the building.

The Guggenheim Museum was one of the places Amelia had mentioned in her journal. She'd never been here, and it was at the top of her list of places she wanted to visit, along with Trump Plaza, Times Square on New Year's Eve, the Cloisters, and Central Park during the annual marathon.

From the looks of her, he'd scored a bull's-eye. Not that he hadn't had help. Reading her journal was like having an owner's manual. He cut his grin short and focused on her. "It's even better on the inside," he said. Although the rain was still a light drizzle, that could change in a minute. He didn't mind riding in a downpour but he wouldn't subject her to it.

She nodded, her eyes alight with excitement. Hard to believe she hadn't been to the Guggenheim. It was one of the most famous museums in the world. He wasn't sure what the current exhibit was, and he didn't care. This wasn't about art appreciation.

She slipped her helmet off as she dismounted the bike, then shook her head and fluffed her hair. It wasn't meant to be seductive, but it was. He wondered if a penis could explode from overstimulation. God, he hoped not.

"I've never been here," she said. "I've wanted to come, but I never got around to it. This is great."

He tried not to look too cocky as he took her helmet and his and walked up the staircase leading to the main entrance.

Inside, Amelia's gaze shot up. It was a natural reaction, and he doubted if anyone but the employees could resist it. The building was round; the ramps to each floor followed the arc. Designed by Frank Lloyd Wright, it was as beautiful as any of the art it showcased.

He paid for two tickets and checked the helmets and their jackets. He'd seen the Warhol exhibit before, but that was okay, because he didn't really want to be distracted. Amelia was what fascinated him, and now he had a nice, quiet space to watch her. Learn about her.

She stopped at one of the first paintings, Warhol's famous *Marilyn Monroe.* As she read the commentary and studied the picture, he studied her.

Her profile made him crazy. Her beautiful hair, little nose, lips almost as pink as her blush. And those eyes. Like a child's. Inquisitive, guileless, trusting. God, to see her eyes the moment of penetration, the moment of climax.

He wanted to see her with a sheen of sweat over

that perfect skin. Riding him as he lay back, watching her.

She walked over to the next painting, but he didn't even bother to glance at it. Something did catch his eye, however. A guy, standing about thirty feet away, checking her out.

He looked like a college student, like one of the regulars at the café. Brown army coat, backpack, jeans, logger boots. His hair fell in his face, and he kept pushing it back. His attempts at subtlety fell flat as he stole glance after glance.

Jay put his hand lightly on her shoulder. She smiled up at him, oblivious to the one-act play even though she was the star. He leaned close to her ear and kissed the soft curve of her neck.

She sighed, and he moved behind her, so close they touched from chest to knees. His hands went to her waist. After a moment's hesitation, she leaned against him, relaxing in his arms.

He kissed her neck again as he rubbed her tummy in slow circles. When her head fell back, he nibbled on her earlobe, stroked her soft skin with featherlight laps of his tongue.

He moved his hands up so his thumbs brushed the bottom of her breasts. It was hard not to sneak underneath her blouse, but he didn't particularly want to get thrown out.

Of course, Amelia had something to say about it. She gasped, put her hands on his, stopping him, pulling him away. "No one can see us," he whispered.

"There's someone at the next picture."

"I know. But the way I'm standing, where we're standing, he can't see when I do this." He moved his hands back into position, so his thumbs just touched the swell of her breasts. The danger made him reckless, but he had to be careful. Not push her too far, too fast. But the feel of her was as enticing as anything he'd ever known. He went back to kissing her neck, teasing her as he grew dizzy from her scent.

She put her hands on his again.

"Amelia," he said, his voice so soft it was barely a whisper. He could almost touch the shell of her ear, he was so close. "Put your hands down, baby."

He felt her shiver. "I can't."

"You can. You can trust me. I won't embarrass you. No one will see."

"How do you know?"

"I'm watching very carefully. Nothing bad is going to happen. I promise."

She didn't move for a long time. He was just about to let it go, when her hands drifted slowly to her sides.

"Good girl," he said.

She jumped a bit, and he almost groaned at his own stupidity. Calling her by her alias from True-Confessions.com wasn't very bright. But after a few nervous seconds, he realized she'd reacted to the name without jumping to any conclusions.

He focused once more, and as he relaxed, so did she. His thumbs made small circles, moving up very gradually. He nibbled her earlobe, and she whimpered softly. Then he looked up, scoped the guy with the backpack.

He'd moved closer. Not close enough to see, but Jay knew the guy understood the nature of what was happening, if not the details. The fact that Amelia had leaned in to him made their relationship clear. He had to give it to the kid—he was persistent.

Enough about him. He wanted this to be exciting for Amelia. Daring, yet safe. He rested his chin on her hair and savored the slight scent of green apples. Finally, his thumbs brushed her nipples. Her breath hitched and she stiffened.

"It's okay, baby."

"You swear?"

"Yes."

"That boy…?"

"He can't see. He wants to, but he can't."

"What if he—"

His tongue circling her ear made her lose her place. He teased her until he knew her agitation had nothing to do with the kid with the backpack.

"Amelia," he whispered again, as her nipples hardened under his thumbs. "That boy isn't watching us. He's watching you. He isn't giving me a thought, unless it's to hope like hell I have a sudden emergency somewhere in the Bronx."

"Why?"

He grinned. "Because, my beauty, he wants you."

She put her hands on his again. "What?"

Jay kissed her gently, moving to the curve where her neck and shoulder met. "He hasn't seen anything but you since we walked in here. If I wasn't here, he would be on you in a heartbeat. He'd talk about art, discuss modernism and its impact on society. But what he'd be thinking about was how he was going to get you to go home with him.''

"Don't tease me."

"I'm not." He moved his hands again, this time more blatantly on her breasts, concentrating on her nipples. He squeezed her gently, then, still through the sweater, took the hard nubs between his fingers.

She jerked against him, her hands pressing his, slowing him down, but not by much.

"Relax," he whispered.

"I can't do this."

"You're not doing anything."

"I'm letting you touch me."

"Where? What am I touching, baby?"

"My…"

"Tell me." He whispered the words but his message wasn't gentle at all.

"My breasts."

"There we go."

She moaned, leaned against him again. "Please."

"Please what?"

"Stop."

"Stop what?"

She squeezed his hands. "Not here."

"Do you trust me?"

She shook her head, and he had to laugh. "Can you try?"

Another long pause. "Yes."

"I promise you, this is private. No one but us knows a thing."

PLAY LUCKY 7 and get FREE Gifts!

HOW TO PLAY:

1. With a coin, carefully scratch off the gold area at the right. Then check the claim chart to see what we have for you — **2 FREE BOOKS** and a **FREE GIFT** — **ALL YOURS FREE!**

2. Send back the card and you'll receive two brand-new Harlequin Blaze® novels. These books have a cover price of $4.50 each in the U.S. and $5.25 each in Canada, but they are yours to keep absolutely free.

3. There's no catch. You're under no obligation to buy anything. We charge nothing — **ZERO** — for your first shipment. And you don't have to make any minimum number of purchases — not even one!

4. The fact is, thousands of readers enjoy receiving books by mail from the Harlequin Reader Service®. They enjoy the convenience of home delivery...they like getting the best new novels at discount prices, BEFORE they're available in stores...and they love their *Heart to Heart* subscriber newsletter featuring author news, horoscopes, recipes, book reviews and much more!

5. We hope that after receiving your free books you'll want to remain a subscriber. But the choice is yours — to continue or cancel, any time at all! So why not take us up on our invitation, with no risk of any kind. You'll be glad you did!

We can't tell you what it is...but we're sure you'll like it! A surprise **FREE GIFT** just for playing LUCKY 7!

Visit us online at
www.eHarlequin.co

NO COST! NO OBLIGATION TO BUY!

NO PURCHASE NECESSARY!

Scratch off the gold area with a coin. Then check below to see the gifts you get!

YES! I have scratched off the gold area. Please send me the 2 Free books and gift for which I qualify. I understand I am under no obligation to purchase any books as explained on the back and on the opposite page.

350 HDL DNKJ   **150 HDL DNJ7**

FIRST NAME   LAST NAME

ADDRESS

APT.#   CITY

STATE/PROV.   ZIP/POSTAL CODE   (H-B-04/02)

Worth **2 FREE BOOKS** plus a **FREE GIFT!**

Worth **2 FREE BOOKS!**

Worth **1 FREE BOOK!**

Try Again!

DETACH AND MAIL CARD TODAY!

The Harlequin Reader Service® — Here's how it works:

Accepting your 2 free books and gift places you under no obligation to buy anything. You may keep the books and gift and return the shipping statement marked "cancel." If you do not cancel, about a month later we'll send you 4 additional books and bill you just $3.80 each in the U.S., or $4.21 each in Canada, plus 25¢ shipping & handling per book and applicable taxes if any.* That's the complete price and — compared to cover prices of $4.50 each in the U.S. and $5.25 each in Canada — it's quite a bargain! You may cancel at any time, but if you choose to continue, every month we'll send you 4 more books, which you may either purchase at the discount price or return to us and cancel your subscription.

*Terms and prices subject to change without notice. Sales tax applicable in N.Y. Canadian residents will be charged applicable provincial taxes and GST.

If offer card is missing write to: Harlequin Reader Service, 3010 Walden Ave., P.O. Box 1867, Buffalo NY 14240-1867

"He knows you're kissing me."

"People kiss in museums all the time."

"But—"

"Shh. Just let it go. Close your eyes. I can feel you trembling. I won't let anyone see."

"Okay," she said. "But please..."

"I promise."

She sighed, and he filled the palms of his hands with her sweet breasts. He shifted his hips to let her know he'd become as hard as her nipples.

Only he heard her moan. Felt her backside rub him in a way that was heaven and hell.

He bent to kiss her again, but he stopped as he saw the boy head their way.

Amelia must have realized something was up, because she tensed, but she didn't stop him. He felt her struggle in her muscles, in her shallow breaths.

He continued to rub her intimately, gauging their position and the kid's trajectory.

She stopped breathing altogether a second before his hands dropped to her waist. The boy walked by, pretended to look at the art, glared briefly at Jay, then headed toward the elevator.

She lifted his hands from her stomach and turned around to face him. "Why did you do that? Was it for me?" She nodded in the direction of the elevator. "Or him."

"Actually, I did it for us—but wasn't it something to know he wanted you so badly?"

"He didn't."

"Why do you think he disappeared like that?"

"He was done with this floor?"

Jay chuckled. "Your radar is broken, that's all."

"Radar?"

"Uh-huh. Your roommates have it in spades."

"You mean guy radar?"

"Yep."

She opened her mouth, then closed it again. "The only reason he was staring was that you were putting on a show."

"Nope. He stared at you before I made a move. He wanted you, babe. He still does."

"That doesn't happen to me."

He raised his right brow.

"Okay, so it did happen with you. But you're the only one."

"Is that so?"

"Yes. Don't you think I'd know if someone was flirting with me?"

"You didn't know it about Brian."

She opened her mouth again. It was really charming. And sexy. But then, everything she did was sexy.

"Brian did not ever flirt with me."

"Uh, yeah. He did."

"When?"

"About the first two months you went to the café."

"No." She waved a dismissive hand. "That's nuts."

"Ask him."

"I will not. I would have noticed."

He put his hand back on her shoulder and guided her toward the next painting. "I saw him do it, baby."

"When?"

He tried to remember the first time, but it had been too long ago. "Sometime last summer. I was fixing his speakers. He went over to you and offered you a refill."

"He does that to everyone."

"No, he doesn't."

"Jay, it's a coffeehouse. Of course he does."

"Actually, his policy is to wait until the customers come to him. Not the other way around."

"I've seen him—"

"Only to you, sweetheart. No one else gets the personal treatment."

"That's impossible."

He grinned, loving this. Knowing she was loving it, too, even though she'd never admit it. "You're right."

Her crestfallen expression made him laugh out loud. "I didn't mean it like that. I meant I was wrong. He has brought coffee to a couple of other people."

"Oh."

"All women."

"Okay."

"Beautiful women."

She blinked a few times, the effort to assimilate what he'd just said evident on her face. She simply didn't get it. She could hide all she wanted behind awful clothes and pulled-back hair, but she couldn't change the basic fact that she was a compelling woman. He could understand how a lot of people missed it. She worked so damn hard at hiding, but anyone who paused for even a few minutes would see.

No, that wasn't true. Men. Men would see. Women wouldn't want to. Ergo, her roommates.

"I don't know what to say to that," she said. "I can't think why you'd lie to me."

"I'm not lying. And I wasn't lying about the kid with the hair in his eyes."

She sighed. Shook her head. "Why didn't I know?"

"That's a good question."

Her eyes got serious on him. "My upbringing was strict."

He nodded, urging her to elaborate.

"My aunt, who is a very kind woman, is also a believer in sin. She raised me the best way she knew how, and that was to make sure I didn't attract any attention. Because we're all susceptible to the devil's work. Especially young girls."

"Do you believe that?"

"Not the same way she does. I believe in right and wrong, and the concept of evil. But I also believe that God made us like this out of love."

"Like what?"

"Deserving of pleasure. Making love feels good for a reason."

He smiled, liking her more and more as each minute passed. "Now, that's what I call a philosophy."

"Don't make fun. It's something I've struggled with."

Putting his arm around her waist, he pulled her

close. "I'm not making fun of you," he whispered, searching those clever eyes of hers. "I think you're remarkable."

"Why?"

"Didn't you believe me before?"

"What do you mean?"

"When I was at your apartment."

She shifted her gaze to somewhere near his nose. "I may be naive but I'm not stupid. I knew what was going on."

"You did, huh?"

"You made your point. You saw how gorgeous Donna and Kathy were, and you wanted them to know you liked me. Mostly, I think you wanted me to feel grateful."

"No. That isn't what happened. I'm the one who's grateful."

She gave him a half smile. "You're like abstract art to me. I know there are hidden meanings, but I have no idea if I'm even close to the mark."

"Don't try so hard. It's not that complicated."

"Of course it's complicated."

He shook his head. "It's as simple as one—" he kissed her on the forehead "—two—" he kissed the tip of her nose "—three." He kissed her mouth, tenderly at first. But the moment she parted her lips, the need that had been banked all day coursed through his veins like a flash fire.

All his intellectual bull, and his noble efforts to rescue Amelia from a life of celibacy fell away like so much sand in the shower. He wanted her. He'd wanted her since the moment he noticed her. He wanted the dance, too, but that was tiny, infinitesimal compared to his raw desire.

His tongue touched hers, and he moaned. She tasted of wintergreen and she smelled of autumn, and he wasn't supposed to feel this way. Not this sharp-edged craving.

He was the one in control. He called the shots, made the moves. And he always held back. The one who cares the least has the power. And he'd always had the power.

He pulled away, let her go. He felt blindsided. Tricked. She couldn't be playing him. Could she?

"What's wrong?"

No. That was crazy. He knew so much about her. Her insecurities, her loneliness. That powerful erotic nature of hers. It wasn't possible that it was a setup.

Whatever he'd gotten himself into was his own damn fault. He just had to be more careful, that's all. Keep a little distance.

"Nothing's wrong." He found her hand and squeezed it. "Come on. Let's go look at some art."

SHE TRIED TO FOCUS on the gorgeous Van Gogh, she really did. But with Jay standing so very close, it was impossible. What if…?

What if this was real? What if it really was destiny? Why was this so *difficult?* Her roommates didn't seem to have any trouble. They went out all the time, and she knew from their conversations that each one of them expected to find Mr. Right, fall in love, get married, etcetera, etcetera. Why didn't she have that kind of blind faith?

It had something to do with the death of her parents, with Aunt Grace—but she was old enough now to base her decisions on her life now, not on her past.

Maybe her roommates believed in love so firmly that they made it happen.

Maybe she was so sure it couldn't happen to her that she couldn't believe Jay no matter what he said.

She sighed.

He rubbed her back, casually, which made it an intimate gesture indeed. She hadn't been touched like that…ever. It felt so very, very good.

She needed to stop analyzing everything. What earthly good did it do? She never truly understood anyone else. People confused her. Men, especially. Oh, she knew all about testosterone, and how it influenced behavior, but there were still many things that completely baffled her. Bathroom humor. How anyone could think that amusing was a mystery. And ogling breasts. What was the big deal?

"Hey."

She looked up, a little startled. She'd been in her own thoughts for who knows how long. "Yes?"

"Do you really find this painting that interesting?"

She'd hardly noticed, and when she looked, she had to laugh. It was a white canvas with one beige stripe. That's it. If it meant something, she didn't know what. "No, I was off somewhere else."

"Where?"

She took in a deep breath, let it out slowly. Before

she answered him, she headed for the next picture—
one of a naked woman...sort of. "I was just thinking
about breasts."

He stopped. Blinked. "Hmm," he said. "What are
the odds?"

She laughed. "I wasn't thinking about them that
way. Well, not directly. Actually, what is it about
breasts? What do you men find so captivating about
them?"

"Um, we don't have any?"

"You have nipples."

"Granted. But our nipples are short and boring."

"Whereas our nipples dance and sing karaoke?"

He grinned at her. "If they did, honey, you'd be
the richest woman in the world."

"But why? Is it a mother thing?"

Jay shook his head. "You honestly think you'll
ever understand men? Don't even go there. There's
nothing to get. Men are simple creatures. They eat,
they ogle, they sleep, they work, and they do it all
again the next day."

"That's not true. Men are very complex creatures."

"Okay, so they've got some hidden depths, but
honey, I guarantee we're talking wading pool, not the
Marianas trench."

"That's ludicrous. What about philosophers? Sci-
entists? Musicians?"

"Not to be too blunt, but every philosopher, sci-
entist and musician you've ever heard about had the

same priority as the guys who bowl on Thursday nights.''

''And that would be?''

''Sex.''

''What about adventure? Discovery?''

''You have any idea how often Columbus got laid? That's got to be the best line ever. 'Come on, baby, and I'll show you a whole New World.'''

She had to laugh. Oh, there was a bit of truth to what he'd said, but she knew too many men who had so much more to them. The one in front of her, for example. ''I think you're a very complex man.''

His brows raised. ''Me?''

She nodded. ''Yes.''

''Nah. I'm just another guy on a Harley.''

''Oh, Jay. What am I supposed to do with you?''

He pulled her back into the warmth of his arms. ''Take it slow and easy, and no one will get hurt.''

''I'm counting on it,'' she whispered, but she wasn't at all sure he heard her. Maybe she didn't want him to hear.

AN HOUR LATER, and they still hadn't gotten off the second floor. In fact, instead of looking at a painting or sculpture, they were standing by the rail, watching the rain pelt the street. Amelia shivered, although she wasn't chilly.

He must have felt it, because his arm slipped over her shoulders and he hugged her to him. She let her head rest on his chest.

"When you're ready," he said, "I'll get you a cab."

"Do you want to leave?"

"Nope. But you have to study."

She hadn't moved a muscle during the whole exchange. Neither had he. It was amazingly comfortable, and she seriously considered standing there for the rest of her life.

Lightning shimmered, but there was no sound of thunder. Her gaze moved to the ground floor, to the people shaking off wet coats and umbrellas, cursing the rain. She didn't mind. In fact, she'd always liked thunderstorms. She liked to lie in bed and listen to the roar of the skies.

Wouldn't it be something to have him next to her? Kissing her? Stroking her thigh, her back? Kissing and kissing, then kissing some more?

He shifted, turning her toward him. "Hey."

"What?"

"I want to take you home."

"Oh."

He cupped her cheeks with his broad hands and kissed her gently on the lips. "I want you in my bed," he whispered, his lips still touching hers.

"Oh."

"Naked."

"Uh-huh."

"Is that a yes?"

The tip of her tongue glided across his upper lip. But she didn't answer. Not out loud. But the way she licked his lips... He lived too far away. He'd never last. In fact, if she teased him one more time with that tongue of hers, he'd do something he'd regret later.

Just as he was about to pull back, she did it again. This time, her tongue darted inside his mouth. He clamped down with his lips, sucked hard, then gave her a dose of her own medicine.

She moaned as they danced a hot tango without moving any other parts of their bodies. While he tortured himself with thoughts of what he was going to do to her.

She took a breath, and he remembered she had school tomorrow. Studying to do. He should let her go, let her get a good night's sleep.

Yeah. Right.

11

HE WALKED HER DOWN the circular ramp, his mind
filled with images of giving her a long leisurely bath,
soaping her from head to toe, concentrating on the
important parts. Listening to the storm outside, and
creating some thunder of his own.

She was so much more than he'd imagined. He
should have guessed when he'd read her intricate fantasies. Her imagination was so vivid, so adventurous.
He wanted to make every fantasy come true. The bike
ride had fizzled, but in her journals several times
she'd mentioned making love in a storm.

He picked up the helmets and the jackets. He asked
her to wait at the door while he got a taxi. No easy
feat in this downpour, but finally, he hailed an empty
Yellow Cab. He waved, and she darted through the
rain to scramble into the back seat. When he bent to
get in, her expression stopped him.

"What's wrong?"

"Nothing." She scooted over.

"Amelia, talk to me."

"You're getting soaked."

He was. He ducked inside, but told the driver to
wait, then turned back to her. "Talk to me."

She didn't for a long while, the slap of the windshield wipers almost masking her sigh. "I don't think I can go with you."

"You don't?"

She shook her head. "Not yet."

He could change her mind. With a touch, a whisper, a kiss. He could get her to say yes. But he wouldn't. He shouldn't even try. He'd thought long and hard about her seduction, and taking her to bed now would ruin half the fun. Unfortunately, his cock didn't listen to reason, and couldn't care less about slow seductions and finesse.

"I'm sorry."

"There's no need to apologize. You just go home and study."

"It's not that I don't want to."

"But...?"

"I can't explain. Except, it's not time yet."

"I understand."

"I guess I'm really not like the other women you date."

He touched her cheek with his palm. "No, you're not. And I'm glad."

Her smile warmed him, and he kissed her gently on the lips.

"I have to warn you," she said. "If you get hit by a bus, I'm going to be really pissed."

He laughed, kissed her nose, struggled not to change her mind. "Good night, Amelia."

She frowned. Crossed her arms over her chest. "Good night."

"Are you pouting?"

"Yes."

"Why?"

"Because being mature sucks."

He kissed her again, hard on the lips, then got the hell out of the cab while he still could. The heavy rain soaked his hair as he pulled out a twenty and gave it to the driver along with her address.

Then he winked and shut the door before everything went to hell in a handbasket.

The rain kept on falling as the cab drove off. He didn't move until the taillights disappeared from view. He just stood there sincerely hoping he hadn't been a world-class dope just now. She'd been close. Close enough for the right word to tip her over.

No. He'd stick with the plan. It was a damn good plan, and it was gonna be worth it. So what if he was stiff as a rod and about to split his pants.

He'd get his bike tomorrow. Tonight, he'd grab a cab, take a shower, and become one with his right hand. Again.

AMELIA CONTINUED TO POUT the whole ride home, even though it had been her decision to say goodnight. It was too soon. And she wasn't sure she could have gone through with it. Not yet. It was just such a good day.

How extraordinary. She felt like the heroine in a fairy tale. A very frustrated heroine. Plucked from obscurity by a dark prince. Unfortunately, now she had to go back to her real life, and the prospect numbed her.

She was treading on dangerous territory. It would be easy to fall for Jay. He was so much of what she wanted in a man. He'd be a wonderful father—

Whoa. Two dates, and she was already thinking about love, marriage, commitment, a family. Pretty soon she'd be writing *Mrs. Amelia Wagner* on all her textbooks. How pathetic!

Her thoughts went back to the museum—standing inside the door while Jay hailed the cab. The guy with the backpack had come out of the woodwork. He'd smiled at her. She could tell he'd wanted to come over, talk to her. Why hadn't she seen it before? What else had she missed in her myopic state? Had Brian really flirted with her?

She didn't like being clueless. Clueless was scary. What if Jay was sending out signals and she missed them? She'd shoot herself if she blew this because of her naiveté.

Her aunt Grace, God bless her, hadn't done her any favors keeping her so in the dark. Amelia hadn't helped matters by continuing to hide. Tabby had told her time and again that life wasn't going to come to her door…she had to go out and find it.

Tabby, however, wasn't shy. Neither were Donna and Kathy. All three of them were extroverts and they couldn't understand how difficult it was for her to meet people.

Perhaps it was time to face up to her fears. How on earth was she going to keep Jay if she wanted to disappear every time she faced something new or challenging?

The cab stopped, and she thanked the driver before getting out and dashing to the door. The rain hadn't abated, and she hoped Jay had taken a taxi home instead of his motorcycle.

As she unlocked her apartment door, she prayed she'd be alone so she could think. No such luck. They were all home, in the living room, watching TV. Three pairs of eyes turned her way.

"You sly devil," Donna said. "Where did you find that tall drink of water?"

"Yeah," Kathy said. "You've been holding out on us. He's gorgeous."

"I know," she said, heading to her room. "He's really nice."

"Who cares about *nice?*" Donna got up and stretched, her cropped sweatshirt baring her flat tummy. "He's a major hottie. Does he have a twin brother?"

"Not that I know of."

"Hey, where you going?" Tabby turned down the sound on the TV. "I want to hear about this guy."

"I'll be back. I just want to change."

Tabby smiled at her. "This is so cool."

She blushed, then darted into the bedroom. It was chilly in the apartment and she pulled out a flannel nightgown. Looking through her drawer, her dismay grew as she realized all her sleepwear was long, old or ugly—and she had no money to do anything about it. She just sighed and headed for the bathroom.

A bath sounded like heaven. She wanted the private time to think, to go over every detail of her day. Tomorrow she would write it all down, but tonight she would just relax and remember.

She turned on the water, added a dash of lavender bath salts. The good part about the tub was that it was large and the water stayed hot for a long time. The bad part was that it took forever to fill. She had time to talk to the roommates, which she didn't particularly want to do. Oh, well.

They had turned up the volume on the sitcom, but as soon as she returned to the living room, the set clicked off.

"Who is this guy?" Tabby asked.

Amelia sat down on the couch, debating a cup of tea. "His name is Jay and he owns the Harley shop next door to the cyber café."

"Owns the shop?" Donna said, giving a significant glance to Kathy.

Amelia nodded. "I've seen him there for a long time, but we just started talking a few days ago."

"Wow." Kathy, who'd been stretched out on the floor, sat up and hugged her knees. "I just can't believe how gorgeous he is."

"You mean, you can't believe anyone that good-looking would want me."

"That's not fair."

"I know, I'm sorry. I just…I don't understand it, myself."

"You looked great today," Tabby said. She stood up, then stretched down and put her hands flat on the carpet. She was amazing. "You should dress like that all the time."

"I don't have any money, remember?"

"You've got three wardrobes here to choose from. And Donna, you just shut up. You've borrowed everything that wasn't nailed down."

"Hey."

Tabby straightened and gave Donna a don't-screw-with-me look.

"Fine," Donna said, but she obviously wasn't thrilled about it.

"I don't want to impose."

Tabby frowned at Amelia. "Knock it off. You're not imposing. We're your friends. We want you to be happy."

Amelia smiled, knowing Tabby was telling the truth about herself. She wasn't so sure about Kathy and Donna.

"When are you going to see him again?" Kathy asked.

"I don't know."

"You didn't make plans?"

She shook her head.

"That's brutal," Donna said, with just a hint of glee. Or not. Amelia didn't want to jump to conclusions.

"He'll call her," Tabby said, her confidence rock solid. "Why wouldn't he?" She came over to the couch and plopped down next to Amelia. "I'd love to meet him."

"I'd like that, too."

Tabby stared at her with pensive dark eyes. "He had to do some convincing, didn't he?"

She nodded.

"That's excellent. I like him already."

"He's very bright. And funny."

"And he really is nice?"

Amelia smiled. "Yeah."

Tabby kissed her on her forehead. "I hope it works out, kiddo. I truly do."

"Thanks."

"Now, go get in the tub before we have a flood."

She'd forgotten the bath. She hurried into the bathroom, although she hadn't needed to. The water was so slow that the tub was only just over half full. It was enough.

She locked the door and undressed, careful with her friend's clothes. Then she lit the five candles she kept in the bathroom and turned off the lights. The room was transformed with the flickering flames, the soft illumination, the tranquil scent. Sighing happily, she stepped into the tub and sank down.

Her eyes closed and Jay's image came to mind. So vivid, she felt she could reach out and touch him. She remembered the feel of his lips on hers, the taste of his tongue. He kissed like her dreams. Better.

Her hand ran a slow trail down her chest, under the water, until her fingers reached the soft patch of curly hair. Lingering there, teasing herself, she fell into her memories.

His touch had been so gentle, and yet so firm. That

was it, of course. The contrasts. The soft skin of his chest covering hard muscles. Oh dear.

This was heavenly torture. It still felt unreal, as if it had been another Amelia. She'd caught him looking at her so often, and each time, she'd been shocked at his intensity. There was no mistaking that he *saw* her. And she saw him.

And what he'd done to her at the museum… touching her so brazenly in such a public place…God, she'd been so embarrassed, and so turned on. How could the two go together like that?

She touched her nipple, the way he had. They were hard already from her thoughts, the air on her damp skin, and she moaned at the sensations that went straight between her legs.

She'd never realized, until right now, how safe her fantasies were. They were all in her head, and they served to get her through the night, but they certainly weren't real life. Nothing could come close to that. He'd only kissed her. Touched her. Making love with him would be an experience she couldn't even imagine.

If she didn't mess up.

No, she wasn't going to think about that now. Now, she was going to believe in herself. In dreams.

Her fingers moved lower, and as she pictured Jay taking off his clothes, she pleasured herself. Tensing, almost there, she stilled her hands, breathed deeply. This wasn't going to be fast; she wouldn't let it be fast.

If this thing, whatever it was, with Jay was going

to happen, she was going to have to get brave. Not just think about being brave. But actually *be* brave.

He was worth it. Even if, in the end, it all crumbled like puff pastry, it would be worth it. Wouldn't it?

Then logic fled as her body demanded one hundred percent of her attention. Heat pulsed, her breath became shallow and fast, and Jay's lips, the feel of his tongue…

No longer able to stem the tide, she quickened her pace, threw her head back in a long, aching keen, and she came. A shuddering climax that was everything and nothing.

She wanted to be with him. She *would* be with him.

JAY FINISHED HIS DRINK and looked around the bar. He came here a lot—too often, maybe. It wasn't a fashionable New York nightspot. More a neighborhood gathering place, mostly for bikers. He knew people here. It was comfortable. Most of the time.

His radar told him there was a woman approaching at six o'clock. Normally, that would have been welcome news. Tonight, he couldn't muster much enthusiasm.

He felt her heat at his arm and turned to her. A dark-haired beauty with big brown eyes. He'd seen her in the bar before, and they'd shared a steamy glance or two. Wouldn't you know she'd make her move now? While he was so busy with Amelia?

Thoughts of Amelia, at least. The urge to call her had pestered him for hours, and he wondered if he could distract himself with the smiling lady at his arm. Maybe. But it wasn't going to happen. He couldn't do it.

Wrong. He didn't want to.

"You look so serious," she said.

He nodded. "Got a woman on my mind."

"Anyone in particular?"

"Yep."

Her smile faded, and she shifted her gaze to the bartender. "Well, good luck."

"Thanks."

She ordered a cosmopolitan and gave Jay one last hopeful look, but she must have seen he wasn't interested. She paid for her drink and left. He didn't even look to see where she went.

Wonderful. He was obsessed. His life wasn't complicated enough? That made him smile. His life wasn't complicated. He had money, the shop was doing well, he wasn't in trouble and he wasn't bored. The only thing complicating his life was his own thoughts.

His father was supposed to come by and pick up some books Jay's grandfather had left for him. Jay strongly considered boxing the books and leaving them with Jasper. But he wouldn't. He hadn't talked to his father in a long time. Maybe the old man had mellowed, now that he'd seen Jay's success with the shop. Doubtful, but possible. Nothing would appease his father but for Jay to go back to school, write another novel. Fit in to his father's life.

Not gonna happen. He was happy. He hated academia. He'd had one book in him and he'd written it already. He just wished his father could accept that.

Jay ordered another scotch, and after he paid for it, he went over to the pool tables and put up a quarter for next game. He hadn't brought his stick, hadn't thought about playing. But a game would get his mind off things.

As he waited for the two college jocks to finish their marathon game, he leaned against the wall and sipped his drink, the heat spreading through him slowly. A woman smiled at him from a chair across the way, and it happened again...he wanted to call Amelia.

He'd tried to stay home. Take it easy. But restlessness had pushed him out the door. At least here the music was good, the pool tables were level, and the scotch was smooth. What more could a man ask for?

Amelia.

He shot back the rest of his drink, slammed the glass down on the closest table and headed for the door. The rain had stopped while he'd been in the bar, and now the air was crisp and clean and cold. His gaze moved up to the skyline, and he just stared at the sight for a long while.

He loved this city. Everything about it. Well, maybe not everything. But a hell of a lot. He fit here. Amelia did, too, although she didn't believe it.

This was a town for eccentricities. For complexity. And she was both of those things. He headed home, but he took his time, enjoying the night. This was making-love weather. Bath weather. Oh, shit. He was right back where he'd started. Thinking about her. Thinking he'd been an ass to let her go. Wondering how long he should wait to call her.

The thought sobered him completely. What the hell was going on here? He was acting like an idiot, and it was going to stop. *Now*.

Sure, she was interesting, and he was attracted to her—but shit, this was about sex. Hot, hard, down-and-dirty sex with a woman who wanted it just as badly as he did. That she didn't know that yet was the game.

He wasn't about to get caught in any kind of relationship. It wasn't his style. Hell, he'd just finished thinking he had everything a man could want, including his freedom.

No way he was going to let himself get crazy over her. Not now, not ever.

He turned back toward the bar. Maybe he could still find that brunette.

12

―――――

THE PHONE RANG, and Amelia's heart stopped. It was probably for one of the others. The only person who ever called her was Aunt Grace, each and every Sunday at eleven forty-five.

She didn't answer it. Tabby and Donna were both home, and they usually raced to be the first to pick up the cellular. She should just get back to her book. It wasn't him.

The ringing stopped. The words in front of her blurred as she waited. The seconds ticked by, and after sixty of them she let go a sigh. It really wasn't him.

Focusing once more on the textbook, she tried not to be disappointed. It wasn't the end of the world. He hadn't said he'd call. As Donna had pointed out, they'd made no—

"It's for you."

Amelia looked up at Tabby approaching from the bedroom door. "For me?"

Tabby's grin told her who was on the line.

Amelia took the phone, trying to control the heat rushing to her face, but it was useless. Even his calls made her blush.

"Hello?"

"Hey."

His voice. Oh God. She melted. "Hey."

"How was school?"

"Fine."

"I went to the café. You weren't there."

"I know. I had to go to work right after class."

"I missed seeing you."

She grinned and hunkered down on her bed. "You did?"

"I have something I've got to do tonight, but maybe tomorrow we can get together."

The sharp stab of disappointment didn't surprise her. All she'd thought about since the moment he left was when she could see him again. "That would be great."

He was quiet for a long time, but she could hear his soft breath. "I'll call you."

"Okay."

"Amelia?"

"Hmm?"

"I had one hell of a dream last night."

"Tell me."

"I will. Tomorrow."

"Okay." She wanted to stay on the phone. To talk to him forever. "Tomorrow."

"Bye."

She hung up the phone and rested it in her lap. He'd called. He wanted to see her again. And, oh, how she wanted to see him. It was great, wonderful, and yet...she'd hoped...

It would give her a chance to finish her book. She needed to iron, too. No big deal.

Only, it *was* a big deal, and when she tried to read, nothing stuck—pages full of words with no meaning. It was only six-thirty, and the night loomed in front of her like an empty cave.

She got up, headed for the kitchen. Tabby was there, making a grilled-cheese sandwich.

"He sounds luscious."

Amelia smiled. "He is."

"Am I going to meet him tonight?"

She shook her head. "He has other plans."

"Oh, man."

"But we're going to get together tomorrow."

Tabby nodded. "So, why don't you come with us tonight?"

"Where?"

"The frat party at Tri Delta."

"Thanks, anyway, but—"

"Don't dismiss it out of hand. You need to get out. If you stay here tonight, all you'll do is drive yourself nuts thinking about Jay. And don't tell me you've got to study. You study more than anyone I know, and you're going to ace every class, and when it's all over and done with you're not going to regret a few hours of lost cramming. But you will regret staying home. Hiding. You've made such a big breakthrough. Why not keep it going?"

Amelia considered Tabby's point. It was true, she didn't have to finish the book tonight. She'd been ready to drop her studies on a dime if Jay had been available. So why shouldn't she go to a party? She'd already made the decision to be brave, and this seemed like a perfect opportunity to be the new her. If she messed up, it wouldn't matter. She didn't know any of the guys at Tri Delta. Besides, if she hated it, she could go home. She turned to Tabby. "All right."

"Excellent. We've got a few hours, so let's figure out what you're going to wear."

Amelia poured herself a soda, and shook her head at her own foolishness. It was a frat party. That's all. She wasn't going to meet the president or sing on national TV. So why was her tummy doing flip-flops?

She was a wuss, that's all. What guy in his right mind would want a wuss for a girlfriend?

Certainly not Jay.

THE MOMENT JAY OPENED his door, he realized his mistake. His father's face was set, hard, determined. He wasn't pleased about being here, wasn't pleased at all.

"Come on in."

His father walked by him, leaving a trail of cherry pipe tobacco. His Meerschaum stuck out of his jacket pocket, as usual. Jay often wondered why his dad had been so willing to be a cliché. At least, thank God, there were no suede patches on the elbows of his jacket.

"You haven't changed anything."

Jay closed the door. "What did you expect? Black lights and lava lamps?"

"So it's to be like that, is it?"

Jay bit back a sigh. It was always like this. Why would tonight be different? "I'll get the box."

Lucas nodded curtly, then went to the bookcase to wait. Jay hurried to his bedroom, anxious to get this over with. He should have made an excuse, left the box outside. Too late now. Hell, too late by about five years.

He walked back into the living room and his gut clenched when he saw the book his father held. Not that. Not again.

"Such talent." His father looked him in the eye. "Such a waste."

"That I didn't write another, or my whole life in general?"

"I think you need to answer that question, Jay. Not me."

"Yeah. Right. Here are the books. There's an envelope there that Grandpa wanted you to have. I don't know what it is. The envelope was sealed."

"I'll look at it when I get home. I don't suppose you've spoken to your brothers lately?"

"Nope."

"You could call, you know."

"I could. So could they."

His father put the slim novel back where he'd found it. "Is your rebellion so important that it will cost you your life?"

"It stopped being a rebellion a long time ago. This *is* my life. The one I want to lead."

His harsh dark eyes narrowed. "Then, I feel sorry for you."

Jay didn't let the words get to him. It was an old tune, one he'd heard a million times. Instead, he looked at the man. His father had gotten so much older since the funeral. Grandpa had hoped for a reconciliation before he died between his son and grandson. It didn't happen. It most likely wouldn't happen.

His father went to the door, the box tucked under his left arm. Before he walked out, he turned one last time. "You are the most brilliant young man I've ever known. You have a gift that is rare and precious. You owe something in return."

"I don't owe a goddamn thing."

"Have it your way."

"I am."

His father walked out without shutting the door. Jay heard his footsteps on the carpet. He even heard the elevator scrape open and shut. Too-familiar anger roiled inside, and he wanted to smash his hand through the wall. The man was so pompous. If it wasn't his way—

Jay stopped. Just put on the brakes. His father was his father was his father. What was anger going to accomplish?

He closed the door, went to the kitchen where he'd started a pot of water for spaghetti. No longer hungry, he turned off the stove and grabbed a beer. Nine-fifteen. Still early.

He went to the phone and dialed Amelia's number.

How could anyone think this was fun? Amelia stood in the corner of the frat house living room, watching the mayhem spread out around her. She couldn't hear anything over the pounding music, yet it was so crowded, no one danced. There was a great deal of raucous laughter, although she'd yet to hear anything funny.

Ten more minutes, and she'd go home. She promised herself she'd stay till ten, no matter what. All she had to do was keep quiet, stay out of the way, and she could make her getaway.

A girl who looked about sixteen stumbled out of the bathroom. She had no top on. Just a bra. The girl was so drunk, Amelia thought surely she'd pass out any second. Evidently, she hadn't been alone in the rest room. A large guy wearing a football jersey over jockey shorts followed her drunken path.

Amelia hugged the wall, not wanting to be near either of them when they fell—or got sick, which was actually more likely. She didn't really have to wait till ten. Nine fifty-two was close enough.

All she needed was to get her jacket from the back bedroom. It wasn't such a simple task. She had to avoid beer mugs, elbows, something on the floor she didn't want to think about, and a flying CD jewel case that nearly poked her eye out.

Mere steps away from the bedroom, someone grabbed her arm. It was a big hand, thick. Too strong.

She turned to a red-faced boy. She recognized him but couldn't remember his name. He'd been at the apartment once, a long time ago. With Kathy? Maybe. He'd been polite, although they'd barely spoken.

"Hey. You're ah…"

"Leaving."

He shook his head. "Emily."

"Amelia. And I am leaving."

"You can't leave yet. The party's just getting started."

"I'm sure you'll have a great time. But I have to go."

"You have to have a beer. This is a kegger. I've been watching you. You haven't even had one."

"I don't like beer."

He looked wounded. "Everybody likes beer."

"Not me." She looked pointedly at his hand, still holding tight to her arm. "Would you let go."

He shook his head. Taller than almost anyone else at the party, he was also built like a tank, and there was no way for her to break his hold. He dragged her into the kitchen. It was packed, and beer had been sloshed everywhere. On clothes, on the floor. The smell was pungent and made her stomach clench.

"Hey, Darren. Give Emily a beer, would ya?"

"It's Amelia, and I don't want a beer."

He ignored her as he downed the contents of his mug in a series of huge gulps. His Adam's apple bobbed and a dribble of beer leaked down his chin. When he finished, he burped so loudly he drowned out the music, then smiled proudly. "Beer, man. It's so great. I love beer."

"I'm glad. Now, please, let me go."

"Not till you've had yours." He pulled her closer to the keg.

His grip hurt. Every time she pulled back, he held

on tighter. She wasn't amused. In fact, she was getting scared. Maybe if she took the drink, he'd let her go.

"This is Emily," he said to the guy at the keg. "She needs a beer."

The boy didn't even look at her. He just poured a great mugful and shoved it in her direction. The oaf holding her arm took the mug. "Come on, baby. Let's go to the couch."

"I have to leave. If you'll just give me the—"

He didn't hear her. Or maybe he did, but he didn't care, because he was pulling her behind him as if she were a pack mule.

Her purse got snagged on the edge of a chair, and she thought her arm would get ripped off while she tried to untangle it. "Would you stop?"

Amazingly, he did. But when she looked up, she knew it wasn't her plea that had gotten through his thick skull. Jay stood in front of him, blocking his path.

"How—?"

"You'd better let go now, buddy."

The bruiser weaved a bit, and his eyes narrowed as he tried to focus on Jay.

"I said let her go."

The party continued without a ripple, but Amelia neither saw nor heard anything but the situation before her. She had no idea how Jay had found her. It couldn't be a coincidence. And while she was grateful and thrilled to see him, she had a very bad feeling about this. The drunk was just the kind of moron who liked to settle things with his fists, and ask questions later.

"Get lost," he said. "She's with me."

"On the contrary," Jay said, keeping his voice as low as possible. "She's not. And you need to let go."

Instead of releasing her, the guy put the mug down on an end table, then stood up as straight as he could, puffing up his chest. He was taller than Jay by several inches, and outweighed him by who knows how much. But one look at Jay's eyes made it clear the kid was out of his league.

He pushed Jay, square in the chest. Jay stumbled back a few steps, then came right back in the guy's face. "I suggest you stop this right now. We don't want this to get ugly."

"You're already making it ugly, just by being here."

Jay smiled, turned his gaze to her and winked. Two seconds later, her arm was free, the jock was bent double, moaning like a sick cow, and Jay had his hand out to her. She grabbed on to him for dear life, and they made it to the front door, accompanied by the sound of retching.

Once outside, the quiet came as a shock. He held her hand gently as he led her to his bike and handed her a helmet.

"Wait a minute," she said. "How did you get here?"

"I called your place. Kathy told me where you were."

"You did?"

He nodded.

"What about your plans?"

"They ended earlier than expected. Now, why don't we get the hell out of Dodge before Hoss in there decides to reassert his manliness."

"Good plan." She put on her helmet, then waited for him to get on the bike.

"You're going to freeze."

"My jacket's inside, and I'm not going back for it."

He nodded. Looked at the frat house for a few seconds, then turned back to her. "Here—" He took off his leather jacket and put it around her shoulders.

"Now *you'll* freeze."

He shrugged. "I'll be fine."

"I see." She put the jacket on properly, his scent mixed with leather more intoxicating than any beer. "So if you're truly a manly man, cold can't touch you."

He grinned. "I'd rather you be warm than me. If that makes me a macho jerk, well, then—"

She smiled back at him. "It makes you very sweet."

His brow furrowed as he mounted the bike. "Hey. Come on. I have a reputation here."

"Sorry." She climbed on behind him, wrapped her arms around his waist and rested her head against his flannel shirt. He revved the motor, and took her off into the cold night. She'd never felt safer.

They drove straight to her apartment. When they got off the bike, she looked at him questioningly.

"I thought you might like to get your own jacket."

"Freezing, are we?"

She could see him flush under the streetlamp. "Yeah."

Chuckling, she led him inside. The elevator ride was brief, and they didn't even touch. Not really. Just a brush of his hand against her thigh. She wasn't even sure there had been contact. But there was no mistaking the heat.

Kathy was home studying, which was quite rare, and only ogled Jay for a few moments. Amelia peeled off his jacket, handed it to him, and got one of Tabby's from the hall closet.

"What now?" she asked as she donned the blue parka.

"Let's go."

Her heart hammering with excitement, Amelia said good-night to Kathy, who smiled as if she wanted them to have left already, and in short order they were back on his bike, heading for adventure.

She could hardly believe it. He'd rescued her with some kind of superhero move, then whisked her away. With every new event, it became more difficult to believe it was happening to her. To say this was outside of her experience was an understatement.

She felt like Cinderella. Like Sleeping Beauty. Like every Disney heroine ever made. And he was Prince Charming.

Of course, she knew he wasn't really. He was human, like everyone else, and he had flaws. But for right now, she only wanted to see the hero in him.

He'd actually fought for her honor! Wait till she wrote *that* in her journal. But she was getting ahead of herself. The evening with Jay had just started. It was entirely possible that what had happened at the party would dull in comparison with what lay ahead.

She squeezed his waist and muffled her laugh on his jacket. Maybe what lay ahead was her getting laid. Holy cow.

His hand still throbbed. Not that he would admit it, but damn, that boy had been a hulk. The only reason the oaf had gone down like that was because of where Jay had hit him, not how hard. He'd studied *aikido* for five years, and he'd used the guy's position and strength against him.

But man, his hand hurt. He hadn't been to the *dojo* in over a year, and it showed.

Screw it. Amelia was safe. With him. And the night was young. He'd take her to his favorite place. They'd talk and laugh, and then he'd see. He wouldn't press her. He didn't think he'd need to.

He sped up. Just a few hours. Then heaven.

13

SHE CLOSED HER EYES as they flew down the street. The roar of the motorcycle masked the sounds of the city. Jay blocked the worst of the wind, so she could concentrate on what was really important. How his hips felt nestled between her knees. The scent of leather. The way his stomach muscles reacted to her teasing touch.

If they'd ridden forever, she would have been happy. Blissful. For this moment, everything in her world was perfect. Of course it couldn't last, but she also didn't want to let it slip through her fingers.

Jay was her dream man. She'd literally dreamed of him for months. She'd fantasized about him in ways that would make him blush. Oh, if he ever guessed at that...she'd die. It didn't matter, though, because this was real. This wasn't words on a computer screen.

She wasn't going to be Good Girl for long.

At least, she hoped not.

What if tonight was the night? What if he was taking her to his apartment? Thank God she'd shaved her legs. And worn her nicest underwear. They weren't exactly Victoria's Secret, but they weren't old lady panties, either. She'd make sure the light was off. And not just because of her undies.

She was scared to death. Excited, yes, but terrified. That's what made everything so tough. If only she could be sure she wouldn't mess things up.

She remembered that night with Kevin, the moment she'd realized he'd fallen asleep. The burning shame. He'd still been inside her. He hadn't come. She hadn't even known how to come with a man. The humiliation was as raw today as it had been back then.

But maybe tonight she could form new memories. Wonderful, hot memories.

Her thoughts turned as Jay rounded a corner. Something she'd written about awhile ago. Before she'd even seen Jay. The fantasy had been so sensual, so hedonistic. In it, she'd been completely free of embarrassment. She'd been confident, at ease with her body and his. And she'd let herself do everything, taste everything, experience it all.

He'd licked her body from her toes to her forehead, skipping nothing. He'd savored her scent, the taste of her, her curves, her soft moans. He'd worshiped her, and when he finally entered her body...she'd been acutely aware that none of it was real.

The disappointment had stopped her in her tracks. Not because she couldn't imagine making love. That part was easy. But in this fantasy, the most intense of her life, she'd been in love and he'd been in love with her.

It still gave her shivers to realize how she'd described Jay to a tee, without ever having laid eyes on him. No, almost to a tee. Her dream man hadn't been quite as handsome. As erotic. And he hadn't had Jay's chest.

They turned another corner and she looked up. She recognized the street. His street. Her pulse sped faster than the bike. This was it.

Show time.

HE LET HER IN the apartment first, glad he'd picked up before his father had come by. Not that the place was a pit, but sometimes he let the papers stack up.

She hadn't asked him yet what his intentions were. But he could tell from her wide eyes that she suspected. And she was right.

He smiled as the door closed behind him. "Make yourself comfortable. I'll be just a few minutes."

She nodded as she went to the bookcase. Interesting. Most of the women he brought here made the liquor cabinet their first stop.

He slipped away, heading to his bedroom and the storage closet. He didn't want to forget anything. It was important that she feel relaxed and comfortable. Maybe it was too cold? No. He'd keep her warm.

First, the blanket. It was thick and soft, and it would fight the chill. A couple of pillows, too. He debated taking the comforter, but decided against it. He grabbed his portable CD player and a flashlight. It took longer than he'd hoped to find the right music, but he wasn't willing to compromise. Easy jazz. Dave Grusin. Antonio Carlos Jobim. He put it all into his army duffel. His gaze caught on the mirror, and his cock jumped, remembering the other day when she'd seen him naked. Dammit. It was too soon to get this hard. The night had just begun. He focused on baseball scores as he headed for the living room.

She had a book in her hands. Open. He peered over her shoulder. Shit, it was his. That wasn't the discussion he wanted to have tonight.

At least he wasn't worried about his hard-on anymore.

She looked up, turned to face him. "This is what Shawn was talking about."

He nodded. "It's no big deal."

"Pardon me? Getting published is a big deal. And from the copyright date, you must have been very young."

"I was, and it shows." He took it from her hand and put it back on the shelf. "Come on. I need your help."

She glanced back once, then followed him into the kitchen. He opened the fridge and pulled out his reserve bottle of champagne. Dom Pérignon. "You like?"

"I have no idea."

"You've never had champagne?"

"Yes, I have. But not good champagne."

"Okay, then. We'll take care of that omission. You hungry?"

She shook her head. "What, exactly, are we doing?"

"You'll see."

"You've got a thing for secrets, don't you."

He grinned. "Yeah. I do."

"It's the drama, I think. The showmanship."

He cocked his head. "It's the least of my quirks, trust me."

"Quirks?"

"Let's just say, the longer you know me, the more you'll discover."

"Oh God. You're not wearing your sister's panties, are you?"

His grin faded, and he opened his eyes as wide as he could, as if his terrible secret had been found out.

Her hands flew to her mouth and her eyes got bigger than his. "Oh, no. I'm sorry. I didn't mean... There are lots and lots of men who like that kind of thing. There's nothing wrong with it, I'm sure."

He couldn't keep it together. Not when she was so earnest. "I'm joking."

"What?"

"I'm not a cross-dresser. You can relax."

She closed her eyes as she exhaled. When she opened them again, he saw she wasn't amused. "You think that's funny?"

He nodded.

"Really?"

He nodded again, but took a prudent step back.

"You have a warped sense of humor, Mister Wagner."

"Quirks. I warned you."

"One of my quirks is that I don't like men with a warped sense of humor."

He put the bottle on the counter and headed straight

for her, his head lowered, trying like hell to look mad. "Now, you know that's not true, don't you, Amelia?"

"It's absolutely true." She crossed her arms over her chest, then she stepped back. Her eyes were alight with humor, with pleasure. He wanted to make her look that way often. At least once a night.

He sighed dramatically. "Amelia, Amelia. Don't you know what happens to beautiful girls who fib?"

"I wouldn't know, because I haven't lied."

He took another step, which backed her up against the counter. He had her now. Nowhere to run, nowhere to hide. He moved closer, invading her space. Her hands dropped and grasped the counter. Her breath quickened; she wasn't quite panting, but was excited.

He had to admit, he was pretty damn excited himself. She was something else.

At the sound of her giggle, his problem rose again. That was a first. He'd gotten hard over lots of things, but never a giggle.

"I can tell you lied," he said, touching her nose with his index finger. "I think your nose got longer."

She looked down at his jeans, at the obvious erection. "Something got longer, but it wasn't my nose." Then her cheeks blushed bright pink and she blinked at her own audacity.

He was a little shocked himself. "That's pretty sassy for a girl who hasn't ever had good champagne."

"Sassy?" She giggled again.

He closed the space between them so that his body,

with his still growing erection, pressed against hers. "Yeah. Sassy."

"I've never been called that before."

"That's because they don't know you."

"Who's they?"

"Everyone else."

"But you do."

He nodded slowly, his humor ebbing as his hunger flared. Their gazes met, as he saw his own desire mirrored in her eyes. The air fairly crackled with unspent energy.

Unwilling to play any longer, he kissed her gently. The cool, impossibly soft lips opened with a tiny sigh that sent her sweet breath into his mouth. The sensation was ridiculously erotic. Intimate. And when she shifted her hips, rubbing his hard length, he used every ounce of willpower not to carry her to the kitchen table and ravish her.

There was a decision to be made here, and with most of his blood busy down south, it wasn't easy. One kiss, the same kiss, only harder now, tongue thrusting in a pale imitation of what would come later, and he pulled back. "Come on," he said, taking her hand.

She moaned, letting him know she wasn't happy about the change in direction, but she didn't fight him. He grabbed the champagne, then got two glasses out of the cupboard and handed the whole kit to her.

He grabbed the duffel and nodded toward the window. "There."

She looked at him, startled. "You want to jump out the window? That's a bit extreme, isn't it?"

He chuckled. "Fire escape."

"Oh. Okay."

He showed her, still chuckling, where to step out the window, and he followed her up the metal stairs, four floors, until they reached the roof.

He held her steady as she stepped over the ledge. He didn't want to let her go, but he had to, or else he'd fall, and that couldn't be good for his sex life.

He hoisted himself over. She was busy checking out the large, flat roof. There wasn't much up there. An antenna, some electric fuse boxes, two beach chairs and an empty plastic wading pool, all illuminated by two weak bulbs hung on either side of the fuses. But that wasn't why he had brought her here.

"Wait," he said, as he made his way to the center of the roof and opened up the duffel. He took out the blanket and spread it out, then the pillows. His CD came next, and he popped in the Jobim.

The Latin jazz was perfect. And so was his companion. He took the bottle and the glasses from her hand. "Look up," he whispered.

She did, and her mouth fell open. It wasn't like being in Manhattan. The stars sparkled in the dark October sky, putting on a dazzling show. The crisp air stirred her hair, made her nose pink, and he wanted her so badly he ached.

"Sit," he said.

She obeyed, curling her legs under her. He popped

the cork, poured her a glass, then one for himself before he joined her on the blanket.

She raised her glass. "To the beauty of the night."

He clicked her glass with his as he held her gaze. "My thoughts, exactly."

They each sipped some champagne. "Oh, my. This is good."

He nodded. "It makes a difference."

"They shouldn't be able to call that other stuff champagne."

He chuckled as he lay on his side, propped up by one hand, his glass in the other. "How come you were at that party?"

She shrugged, but her gaze moved from his.

"If you don't want to tell me, that's okay."

One quick glance, then away again. "No, I don't mind. It's just a little embarrassing."

"Oh?"

She took in a deep breath and let it out. He could see the vapor around her, despite her recent sip of cold bubbly. "I went because I didn't want to."

He blinked. "Run that by me one more time."

"I went because I'm tired of being scared."

"Ah. That makes more sense."

"But I was right to be scared, wasn't I? What if you hadn't come along?"

"Hmm. I'm glad I was able to help, but you would have been able to handle him by yourself."

"That's not true. If I could have, I would have."

"That could have happened to anyone, Amelia. It

wasn't just you. He was drunk and an asshole. They're everywhere, like mosquitoes in summer.''

She held her glass with the tips of her fingers and stared at the liquid inside. "I was scared."

"Which was appropriate."

"You don't get it."

He sat up, moved next to her on the blanket. "Explain it to me."

She didn't say anything for so long that he thought she wasn't going to. Then, in a voice almost too soft to hear, she said, "I've always been this way. Well, at least since my parents died."

"When was that?"

"My mother, when I was eight. My father, when I was twelve."

"Shit."

"Yeah. I just got scared, I suppose."

"Who wouldn't?"

"You."

"You don't know that."

"I see who you are, and scared isn't part of that."

"Not in the way you mean, but believe me, I've got my fears."

"Are they anything like your quirks?"

"Ha-ha."

"I thought it was funny."

He brushed some hair off her cheek. "Go on."

"My mother died of cancer, and my father died of cirrhosis of the liver. Actually, he died of alcoholism. I went to live with my aunt Grace right after my mother died. I told you before, she's a very strict woman who has enough quirks for all of us. But she loves me, and she gave me a good, stable home.''

''But?''

''But I couldn't talk to her about much. Religion. Housework. Nothing personal, though. And because I was so shy, I didn't have a lot of friends to confide in.''

''It must have been tough.''

She gave him an ironic smile. ''You have no idea. I was so ignorant about everything, but especially about, you know, boys and girls.''

''You were. But you're not now.''

''It's not as bad. I know what goes where, at least.''

''Thank God.''

She poked him in the ribs. ''It's not funny.''

''No, it's not. I'm sorry. I can imagine how difficult it was.''

''Probably not, although you do have a vivid imagination.''

''Why do you say that?''

''Look where we are.''

''Point taken.''

''You don't see the dingy roof or the sea of antennas. You see the stars, the romance.''

He nodded. ''I suppose.''

''I have a vivid imagination, too, but it wasn't up to the task of sex. Of course, when I finally did learn a thing or two, I made up for lost time.''

His brows went up, and she clapped her hand over her mouth. ''No, that's not what I meant. Not really.

My imagination went into overdrive, not my...you know.''

"I have a good idea."

"I'm not a virgin, if that's what you're thinking."

Actually, he was surprised. He had been thinking just that. But she clearly thought it was important that she wasn't. "I think it's great that you're not a virgin."

"You do?"

He pushed back his hair with frustration. "I don't know. Should I be? I'm not on very solid ground here, Amelia."

She waved her hand dismissively. "Oh, never mind. It's not important, and it's certainly not your problem."

"What if I told you I want it to be my problem?"

"Jay, it's pretty clear you haven't been a virgin for a long, long time."

God, she cracked him up. "That's not what I meant and you know it. I'm talking about getting to know you. Getting to know each other."

"Yeah?"

He nodded.

"Okay, then, it's your turn."

"What?"

"Confess something."

"Why?"

"Because I did. Now you have to."

"That wasn't a confession."

"No?"

"All right. So it was. But I don't have anything to confess."

It was her turn to laugh. "Right."

He felt his cheeks heat. It must be catching. "Let me think."

"I'm sure it's a stretch."

He poked her in the ribs this time. She just laughed.

"I lost my virginity at fourteen. With my piano teacher."

Her mouth dropped open. "You did not."

He nodded.

"Your piano teacher? Oh my God. My piano teacher was sixty-two!"

"Mine was twenty."

"Better. But still. What a perv."

"I didn't mind."

"You were too young and full of hormones to mind."

"Some things don't change."

"Did you just switch the subject?"

He nodded.

Her eyes narrowed as she studied him in the diffuse light. "Are we going to kiss?"

He nodded again.

"Are you going to seduce me?"

He leaned over and nipped her earlobe. "I'm going to give it my best shot."

"Cool."

He laughed, but only until his lips touched hers. Then it wasn't funny.

It was magic.

14

AMELIA'S EYES fluttered closed as Jay teased her mouth open. The pressure stayed featherlight as their breath mingled. Slowly, he moved his lips back and forth, rubbing hers…not a kiss so much as a moment of transition from the ordinary world to a place outside time and space where every sense was magnified.

He radiated warmth in contrast to the chilly air, and she wanted him closer. Her hand slipped behind his neck. He responded to the message and laid her down on the blanket, her head on a pillow, then curled up next to her so close their bodies touched from lips to toes.

His kiss deepened, and the need to feel him, as much of him as she could, made her want to take off her jacket…and everything else. But for now, it was enough to feel the jolt of his tongue touching hers, the softness of his hair.

Perhaps the most wonderful thing of all was how easy this was. Somewhere between her first sip of champagne and his kiss, she'd given up the fight. This was her life. Her moment. Her man.

His tongue delved deep and slow, and a memory slipped through her sigh. She'd been twelve, and she'd dreamed about kissing. Perfect kissing. She'd awakened in her bed and yearned to kiss a boy—one particular boy named Ethan from her class, who had flaxen hair and startling blue eyes. And then she'd thought how nice it would be to kiss her own mouth, to know what it would feel like when Ethan kissed her.

In a vague, almost guilty way, Jay's kiss was like that. So perfect, it was as if she'd designed his lips, worked with him forever so that he could pleasure her *just so*.

Was it like that for him?

She pulled back, looked at his eyes, so dark and intense with desire. She could look at him forever. He had a different idea, however, and he pulled her into another kiss. Or maybe it was the same kiss, and all the kisses for the rest of her life would be this one kiss. This perfect kiss.

His leg slipped over hers and she felt the pressure of his erection on her leg. So hot and insistent. All for her. Because of her. She thrust her hips, not a lot but enough to make him groan.

"Amelia," he whispered. "God, I thought we'd be safe up here."

"Safe?"

His head rested on his arm, inches away from her own. "I thought it would be too cold. That I wouldn't want to take off your clothes. I was wrong."

She hesitated. With two fingers she stroked his cheek, his strong jaw. "We can go downstairs."

His brow furrowed. "Are you sure?"

She shook her head. "I'm not sure about anything except that I want to be with you. I want to know everything about you."

"You will. God, I want to make love with you."

She sighed and curled into him, letting her head rest on the crook of his neck. "I've never felt this way before. It's…perfect. I'm not sure—" She closed her eyes, not quite believing she had the nerve to say the next few words. "I'm not sure, but I think I'm falling in love with you."

His body stiffened. Not much, but enough. *Oh God.* She'd done it now. Said too much. He'd never said anything about love. Why did she have to open her big mouth? She shifted, wanting to leave, but his arm slipped behind her neck, and he held her close.

"Hey, where do you think you're going?"

"I'm sorry. I shouldn't have—"

"It's okay. It took me by surprise, is all."

"I didn't mean to embarrass you."

"I'm not. I just think that maybe we're getting ahead of ourselves."

"We?"

He nodded. "Yeah. I think we both want things to happen too quickly. We're just getting to know each other. We can afford to take it slow."

She tried to relax again, but everything had shifted. The perfect moment had gone. The night seemed colder, the ground harder. "I'm sorry," she whispered.

"For what?"

"I don't know. For saying that."

"It's okay. I'm flattered."

She groaned and rolled away, escaping from his hold on her. "That's two seconds away from 'We can still be friends.'" She got to her knees, then moved the champagne so she could stand.

"Amelia, don't."

"Don't what?"

He sat up, took her hand. "Don't worry so much. It is what it is. We're here, together. There's no place on earth I'd rather be. You're beautiful, and funny and smart, and this is great right now. Tomorrow will be here soon enough."

She put her hands in her pockets. She'd been so warm in his arms, and she felt so cold now. "I don't know how to do this," she said quietly.

"You don't know how to do what?"

"This. Between us. Whatever it is. I've never done it before."

"I haven't, either."

She laughed. "Come on, Jay."

"It's true. I've never been right here before. Not with you. This is all new. Uncharted territory. I just want to walk through it, not run."

She sighed. "Yes. Of course, you're right."

"It's not a question of right or wrong."

He leaned over and took her face in his hands. How could he be so warm? "You aren't wrong. I never want you to think that. This has been incredible. Everything. Including the fact that I've been more frustrated with you than I can ever remember."

She closed her eyes. "I'm sorry. I don't mean to be frustrating." His laughter snapped her eyes open. "What?"

"Not that kind of frustrated." He put his hands down, rocked back on his heels, then looked at his fly.

"Oh."

"Yeah."

"Well, that's okay."

He laughed again. "Thanks a lot."

She smiled a little. "You still want…" She nodded in the general direction of his jeans.

"God, yes."

"Oh."

"But I can wait."

She stood up. Wrapped her arms around her waist and shivered.

"Let's get inside," he said. "It was crazy coming up here. Too damn cold."

He bent to get his CD player, but she stopped him. "It wasn't crazy. It was wonderful."

Then she was in his arms, and his lips took hers and, what do you know, it *was* the same kiss. The tension in her shoulders melted and the knot in her stomach eased as she felt the truth of his words. There was time. He wasn't going anywhere. Neither was she. But just to make sure, she moved against him. He'd told her the truth.

He still wanted her.

THE WARMTH IN HIS APARTMENT was a welcome relief. He hadn't realized how cold it had gotten till he stepped inside. Amelia must be freezing. "How about something hot to drink?"

She nodded, rubbing her hands together. "Please."

"Tea? Coffee?"

"Either one."

"Okay. Make yourself comfortable. I'll be right back." He left her in the living room and put on a kettle of water. Just as he turned on the stove, a flash of panic shot through him. He'd printed out several of Amelia's confessions. Shit. He thought he had them all in the drawer, but what if he didn't? She was awfully quiet. Dammit, why hadn't he thought to get rid of that stuff? Probably because he took it to bed with him.

He headed for the living room, afraid to see where she was. At least she wasn't at his desk. A few more steps, and he relaxed. She was at the bookcase again. Thank God. "I'm making tea," he said.

She turned, gave him a smile that assured him further. "You have such eclectic taste."

"A lot of things interest me."

She looked up at the shelf. "A book on influenza epidemics, Auden's poems, Stephen King, Dickens, a Far Side Compendium and—" she turned her head a bit to read the title "—*The Art of War*."

"Yeah," he said. "Sounds like me."

"I could spend months here, reading every one."

"You have a favorite book?"

She nodded. "Several. *Prince of Tides. Shogun. Pride and Prejudice.*"

He went to his desk and did a quick visual check. Hell. Right there on his keyboard, a printout of a fantasy. A damn good fantasy where she was tied up and helpless. While she was still engrossed in books, he grabbed the paper and stuck it under the *Wall Street Journal*. He searched again, and didn't breathe until he knew the coast was clear.

"Why didn't you want to talk about your book?"

"It was a fluke. A one-shot deal."

"So? That doesn't diminish the fact that you wrote it, and it got published."

The water should be boiling by now. "Earl Gray all right?"

She nodded. "You're changing the subject again."

"I gotta get the tea."

"Fine. I'll be here when you get back."

"You're a tough cookie."

"Oh, yeah. People quake when I walk in a room."

He grinned as he left her. "Honey?" he said, over his shoulder.

"Yes?"

"No. I meant honey. In your tea."

She laughed, and it was nice because the sound was natural, easy. Not embarrassed at all.

"Yes, honey would be good."

"Don't go away."

"I wouldn't dream of it."

As he got the tea together, he thought of ways to change the subject. He didn't like talking about his book. He'd much rather discuss something worthwhile. Sex, for example.

Although there was a certain appeal about discussing the book with Amelia. Why not? He certainly knew enough secrets about her.

She was on the couch when he came back with the tray. They didn't talk while they fixed their mugs. When all the busywork was done, he leaned back, glad to see she had made herself comfy with her legs curled under her. She'd taken off her jacket, too, which made him happier still.

"The book," she said.

"You're relentless."

"I'm interested."

Hard to argue with that. He sipped some tea as he made his final decision. Screw it. It was no big deal. "I wrote it when I was seventeen. Actually, I started it at sixteen. It got published a year later."

"That's amazing. At sixteen I was struggling with reading books, let alone writing them."

"You weren't. I can tell. You love books too much."

She lifted her brows. "We're not talking about me."

"Right." He turned to look at the small volume in the black dust jacket. "Most of the time it feels like someone else wrote it. Not me."

"Do you think it's just because you're older?"

"No. I think it represents a way of life I turned my back on."

"What way of life?"

"My father's. He's a professor at Cornell."

"Of what?"

"English literature."

She smiled. "He must be so proud of you."

Jay didn't expect the pain in his gut. He kept his face expressionless. This wasn't something Amelia needed to see. "Yeah, he is." The lie tasted bitter, and even the tea didn't help.

"So you were going to be a professor?"

"No. I was going to be the next great American novelist. Only, I couldn't."

"Why not?"

He shook his head, aching to get out of this conversation. "I just don't have any more books to write."

"Hmm."

"What does that mean?"

"Just hmm."

"Liar."

She grinned as she put her cup on the coffee table. "I like your place. It's comfortable."

"Yeah. It is. You would have liked him."

"Your grandfather?"

He nodded. "Great old guy. Full of piss and vinegar."

"What did he think about your life choice?"

"Nice way to put it. He was disappointed, but he understood I had to go my own way."

She caught his gaze. "I don't know if I'm way off base, but... I keep thinking you miss it."

"What?"

"Writing."

He stood, got her cup and his and went to the

kitchen. She *was* off base. He didn't miss the agony of writing page after page of crap. "You hungry?"

"Nope."

After he rinsed out the cups, he came back to her—only, she had her jacket on. "Hey, I'm sorry. I'm an ass. Don't go."

"It's late. I still have to study, and I have work tomorrow afternoon."

He nodded as he grabbed his jacket. "Come on. I'll get you a cab."

"Jay?"

"Yeah?"

She walked to him slowly until they were inches apart. "I got your book from the library."

He rolled his eyes. "Oh, no."

"But I didn't read it. I wanted to ask you first."

"Why?"

"Because it's so personal. I know I'll see a lot of you in your words. Maybe a younger you, but I'll see you differently. I'd never want to intrude, unless I knew you were okay with that."

He cursed himself while he forced a smile. "It's fine. There's nothing to see. It's words on a page. It isn't me."

She touched his cheek. "I think it is. It came from your heart."

He opened the door, ignoring the look of surprised disappointment as he backed off. He'd apologize later. Tell her it was all his fault.

The ride down was silent, and he left her in the lobby while he went outside to hail the taxi. When he snagged one, she walked out slowly, sadly. Fuck it. He'd blown it. She'd never want to see him again, and that was probably for the best. It was a stupid plan, anyway.

She got to the door of the cab, and he stepped back. He should kiss her. It wasn't her fault. He touched her hand, then pulled her into his arms. The moment his lips touched hers, it all shifted inside. He was climbing the roller coaster, every second another inch up.

Then she really messed things up. She put her hand on his chest and trailed it down his stomach. He knew where she was headed, and God help him he couldn't have stopped her if his life depended on it.

She touched his belt, and then, with one finger, drew a line down the curve of his cock. Pulling out of the kiss, she nipped him in the ear. "Next time," she whispered. "I don't think I can wait any longer."

He couldn't move. He could hardly breathe, and when she cupped him, he let out a long slow breath, trying like hell not to grab her and drag her back upstairs.

"I'll dream about you," she said, seconds before she ducked under his arm and climbed into the back seat of the taxi.

Jay stood there for a moment, stunned that he could be this hard this fast. Especially after he'd been so pissed off. What was she doing to him? This was nuts.

"Hey, buddy, you want to give me back my door, or what?"

The cabby's voice shook him out of his trance. He

paid the man and gave him Amelia's address. She
waved as they drove off, but he didn't go back up.
Instead, he walked. He wasn't sure where he was going. It didn't matter. He needed to think.

He presses me against the wall of his bedroom,
raises my legs so that they encircle his waist. With
his two strong hands he shifts my buttocks and
slowly, teasingly, rubs my crotch against his hot,
stunningly erect cock. His mouth finds mine and our
two eager tongues grapple wetly and fiercely; he
wins, swallowing me up entirely. I have not been
kissed this way before.

We don't say a word. Our eyes, fixed on each
other, say it all. His smolder, filled with passionate,
heavy desire, as he lifts my hips and impales me on
his stiff shaft, penetrating me to the very core of my
being, taking possession as if it is his right. I cry out
with the suddenness, the wonder of it, but he hasn't
hurt me. I have the fleeting imagine of a hot knife
cutting through butter. I am the butter, melting on
impact.

He is in complete control of the situation, watching
my face intently as he lifts my hips up slowly and
brings them down in a rhythm that increases in
tempo, his tempo. He moves away from me a bit so
he can lick my aching nipples with his warm, wet
tongue. Ecstatic to be brought to life, finally, after
years of dormant longing, my nipples become hard.
Waves of feeling run down my torso, from my
breasts to my pussy, hard tingles of excitement I can

barely contain. My long pent-up passion rocks me from within. I feel as if I'm falling into a void, my only reality the strong arms and legs of my lover, J.

The pressure builds and then I come, and I come, and he thrusts into me desperately, as if he'll die if he doesn't fill me completely, and my hands, in a frenzy, claw at his shoulders and rake his broad back. And still I come, and never want to stop coming. I tremble and shake and can't stop, not even when, finally, he erupts inside me with a feral scream that goes to the ends of the universe. He holds me close and tight as the last wave crashes over me and I cry out against his hand cupping my mouth, fulfilled, filled to bursting. I have waited such a long time.

Amelia looked up, embarrassed, from her computer, certain everyone knew what she'd just written and how it had excited her. But no one looked her way. Why would they? It was only ten in the morning, and the café had just four customers.

She glanced back at Brian; she was shyer now than ever knowing he found her attractive. But he was busy, too, pouring a cup of coffee for a gorgeous redhead by the copy machine.

She looked at her monitor again, stunned at the power of the words and the thoughts, and how she wanted him. Jay. He'd been upset last night. A week ago, she would have taken that as rejection, hidden behind a bundle of clothes two sizes too big. But today, she saw it differently. He'd become upset because they'd gone too close to an uncomfortable truth. She knew that because she recognized her own discomfort.

He'd told her, that day at the museum, to trust him. And even though it scared her to death, she had. And she still did. He would be there if she fell. He would kiss her and make her better.

And she would be there for him.

So unexpected. This feeling of power. So new and thrilling that she felt like laughing out loud. He hadn't made her strong. He'd helped her to see that she already *was* strong.

She glanced at the words on the screen. Then she clicked the little X in the upper-right corner. When the prompt appeared, "Do you want to save this file?" she clicked No.

15

JAY PRESSED THE OFF BUTTON on his phone and continued to stare out the window at the street below. Mrs. Ashcroft, who lived on the fourth floor, was walking home from the corner market. Mrs. Ashcroft had turned eighty-five on her last birthday, and her body had decided long before that to stop playing fair.

She had what his grandfather called a dowager's hump. Now they just called it osteoporosis. Her back was so bent, she had to crane her neck forward and up just to see in front of her, trusting her wobbly cane to direct the next step.

She went to the store every afternoon at five. She bought a tin of cat food for Twinkles, her obese Siamese, and a little something for her own dinner. Usually a small piece of fish, or a can of sardines with saltines. The woman had been married fifty years before her husband died of a heart attack, and she'd been alone ever since.

She was one of the happiest people Jay had ever met.

He talked to her often. She loved company, loved to laugh. Thought he was the most gorgeous thing to come down the pike since Rudolph Valentino. He'd asked her, one day, when he'd finished taking out her trash, what her secret was. She'd told him.

Passion.

It had made all the difference in her life. Of course, she had to pay attention to the mundane, who didn't? But when it came to the big things—who she would marry, her children, her work, her politics—she used one barometer only. Was she passionate about it? Would she ache if it were gone? Would she fight for it?

He'd asked if having such strong passion didn't make it worse when the passion ended.

She'd shaken her head on her bent neck and told him there were prices to pay for everything, including indifference and apathy. She'd rather pay the price, she said, for having loved.

Today, by the time he focused again, she'd made it past the front steps. Jay walked to his desk, stared at the notes he'd taken. It wouldn't be difficult to get into Cornell. He'd already been admitted. It would be trickier to get into NYU. He'd have to get his transcripts, and fill out the application, do the essay, all that crap.

He wasn't even sure he wanted to go back. Hell, he wasn't sure about much.

He put down the phone and found his mouse, instead. He went to his Favorite Places, and clicked on TrueConfessions.com. But when the familiar logo came on the screen, he didn't log on. Instead, he closed the program, went into his stored files, and started deleting page after page of someone else's life.

AMELIA DIDN'T KNOCK YET. She tugged her skirt, but the darn thing was still indecently short. It wasn't her skirt, of course, she'd borrowed it from Kathy, along with the white knit top, her earrings and a tennis bracelet. Her hairstyle and makeup were courtesy of Tabby's wizardry.

Amelia had actually been pleased when she'd looked in the mirror just before leaving. She wanted to look nice for Jay. Especially because she hadn't seen him in two whole days.

His invitation to dinner had come yesterday, and she'd been in a tizzy ever since.

The thought of how she'd left him three nights ago, the promise she'd made... The idea that they were going to make love was almost more than she could take.

She'd given the matter a great deal of thought. If it didn't feel right, she would honor that. He'd understand. The evening would reveal itself, and she had to trust she would know what to do.

Which sounded great on paper, but the truth was, she wanted to have sex with Jay. More than she could say. The thought of being that close, taking him inside her, gave her goose bumps.

She knocked, and in two seconds the door opened.

The sight of him in jeans and a dark gray shirt changed her. Her cheeks heated and suddenly there wasn't enough air. When he smiled, she melted.

"Hi," she said, feeling a moment's shyness.

He smiled. "Amelia," he whispered. He looked at

her face, not at her short skirt or her makeup or hair. Just her. And there was happiness in his gaze.

She sighed as he pulled her into his arms, into the safest circle of warmth, wrapping himself around her like a cloak. His scent, already imprinted forever, smelled like home.

For a minute they didn't move, except to rock gently back and forth. He held her tightly, almost too tightly, but she didn't mind. Two days apart had given her time to think. To ask herself what she wanted, who she was.

He pulled back just enough to kiss her. Gently at first—a reacquaintanceship. His lips parted, his tongue slipped inside her mouth, and suddenly it wasn't gentle anymore.

He thrust in, hungry, needful, aggressively male. His hands went to the sides of her face as if he was afraid to lose her. Moaning into her mouth, he drowned her in his kisses, filled her with his passion.

When he finally released her and she met his gaze, they both had to catch their breath.

He stepped back, widening the door so she could enter. As she passed him, he touched the small of her back, making her shiver.

After dropping her purse and jacket, Jay kissed her again. No tongue—just hello. "You want a drink?"

She nodded.

"I've got white wine. Come on."

He led her to the kitchen. Way before she got there, a heavenly scent made her aware that she hadn't eaten since morning. She murmured approval, and he grinned.

"It's ready whenever we are. Chicken, baked potatoes, green beans."

"You cook, too?"

"Not exactly."

"Oh, that's right. Shawn said it wasn't your, uh, forte."

"Hey, I can't be great at everything."

She laid her palm flat on his chest. "As long as you're great at the right things…"

He chuckled, then turned to get the wine, but not before she saw the flush on his cheeks. Well, what do you know? Bad-boy extraordinaire Jay Wagner had blushed over a sexual innuendo she'd made. What a rush. She wanted to do it again.

She let her gaze move up his body slowly, until she caught his eye. "I know what I want for dessert," she said, then blinked at her forwardness. What had he done to her? Where was shy, I'd-rather-die-than-be-teased Amelia?

"You do, huh?"

She nodded.

"Damn, I hope you don't mean chocolate cake."

She grinned. "So, you said you'd tell me about yesterday."

He nodded and poured the wine. After handing her a glass, he nodded toward the living room. As she passed him, she ran her hand across his back. She felt brave. More daring than she'd ever believed she could be. She loved what she was when she was with him.

It was incredibly erotic, and she wanted more. She wanted all of it.

"It wasn't a big deal," he said. "I had to go to Connecticut to pick up a bike."

"I'm sorry I wasn't able to go."

"Me, too. I still owe you a ride."

"Don't worry," she said. "I won't let you forget."

He sipped his wine, studied her as she walked to the window. She'd thrown him, she could see it in his expression. Did he have any idea how turned on she was? Her gaze slipped down to his pants.

Oh.

Jay caught her checking him out. He put his glass down, afraid he'd spill it. He still wasn't used to this Amelia. But he liked her. A lot.

This was the woman from her journals. The writer of the hottest fantasies he'd ever read. Okay, so maybe he shouldn't have read her journal, but he couldn't say he was sorry. Not tonight. Not watching the way she held herself. Confident. Sexy. Powerful.

He wanted her more than ever. But he had to let her make the first move. Despite her big talk, he still wasn't sure she'd want to take it to the next level. He could only hope, and pray that if she didn't, he'd survive.

He sat down, wanting her to join him, but she stayed at the window. His gaze moved down her body, and lingered when he got to the soft swell of her behind. Patience had always been his strong suit when it came to women. But not with Amelia. He remembered one of the first things he'd read in her journal, the first time he'd realized he was the star of her fantasies. *So sex has a name.*

AMELIA FELT HIS GAZE on her, felt his pull, but she needed to slow things down a bit. This was major, and it was her call, and she was going to do it right.

She focused on the street, the people five stories below. So many of them. Not like rush hour, but more than she'd have guessed at eight. Coming out of the subway, standing in line at the pizza place, talking on cell phones. All of them oblivious to the inescapable fact that she was about to have sex.

She shifted her vision from the street to his reflection in the window. The look on his face made her squeeze her legs together.

She put her glass down on the window ledge, then leaned forward, her hands on the thick-painted white windowsill. She moved her legs shoulder-distance apart, and let her head droop forward, her hair hanging down in long waves. She closed her eyes and listened to the New York night bustling and wailing. Then she listened to him. His hot heavy breath telling her he'd noticed how very short her skirt was, and how incredibly available she was for the taking.

Part of her wanted to stop. To have dinner, like the good girl she was supposed to be. Flirt a little, chat a little, then make out on the couch until they couldn't take it anymore. After all, the bed was the logical place to make love for the first time.

The rest of her wanted to be bad. To be the woman in her fantasies. He was the only man in the world she'd ever dare this with. He gave her permission. Or perhaps she just gave herself permission.

It didn't matter. She wasn't even sure she could pull it off, but dammit, she wanted to try. All those nights in her lonely bed, dreaming of seduction and sex. All those mornings she'd gone out with her hair pulled back, no makeup, and those big, awful clothes.

No more hiding. No more blending in with the woodwork. She wasn't sure what would happen next, but she was sure that no matter what, she wasn't going to let fear stop her.

"Amelia?"

"Hmm?"

"What are you doing?"

His voice seemed closer. She looked at his reflection, and sure enough, he now stood at the edge of the couch, about five feet away. "I'm watching."

"I see."

"No, you don't. You can't see from all the way over there."

His low chuckle made her bite her lower lip. God, she wanted him. And God, she was scared.

He didn't make a sound as he walked up behind her. She tensed, anticipating his touch. Aching to feel him. Her gaze moved to her nipples, hard underneath the knit top. *Touch me.*

Her lips parted when his hand snaked around her side and pressed into her belly. The other hand slid up her spine to the back of her neck, holding her steady. "What are you doing to me?"

"You already asked me that."

He rubbed against her, showing her just how her little game was affecting him. "This is what you're doing."

She rubbed him back. "I know."

"If you don't stop—"

She turned around, dislodging his hands. "I don't want to stop."

"Amelia—"

She put her hands on her tummy, then moved them slowly toward her breasts. His gaze shifted, and she watched his eyes dilate as her palms moved to her nipples. "I want this," she whispered.

"Oh God."

She moved her fingers to the hard little nubs, and squeezed them. If he didn't do something soon, she was going to faint.

She needn't have worried. He brushed her cheek with his knuckle, then his hand was next to hers on her breast. His eyes closed as he touched her, but they snapped open when he felt her tug at his belt.

"Are you sure?" he asked, his voice a gruff whisper that sounded like sex.

She nodded. "You can't imagine."

"Oh, I can."

She leaned forward until her lips were close to his ear. "Don't you dare be nice," she whispered.

He took hold of her arms and pushed her back so he could see her face.

She nodded. Yes, she was sure. Yes, she meant it. And yes, he'd better do it right now.

He pulled her into a kiss that bruised, that set fire

to her insides. His hand went back into her hair—only, this time, the gloves were off, and he held her steady and took possession of her body.

While he kissed her, his other hand moved down her hip to the hem of her ridiculously short skirt. Hot fingers touched her inner thigh, then slid to rub along the crotch of her panties, as if she were his pet cat.

His tongue thrust deep and hard, and he slipped those same fingers inside the rim of her panties. Time slowed as his finger eased into the slipperiness between her warm lips. Her heart raced and her breath grew shallow as she whimpered with pleasure and relief. He found her clit unerringly, and began slow, perfect circles designed to bring her to her knees.

He pulled back from the kiss, still holding her by the hair. "Take off your shirt, Amelia."

Just hearing him say the words in that husky voice made her tremble, and immediately obey. He let go of her hair, but not her sex.

She pulled the shirt off, dropped it where she stood. His gaze moved down to her bra—white satin, with a clasp in front—and his lips curved into a wicked smile.

"Show me," he said.

"What?"

"What you want me to see."

She sighed, not just from his sly touch, but from the way he understood her. Nothing had ever been this hot. This thrilling.

She cupped her breasts, then flicked her own nipples still underneath the satin bra. His nostrils flared as she found the clasp and eased it open. She didn't bare herself yet. His finger on her center stopped moving. She frowned, looked at him. And his look explained the game plan.

She peeled back her bra, revealing her pale breasts with their hard, aching nipples.

His finger resumed its maddening circles. Her head fell back as she let the bra slide down her arms.

"Touch them," he said.

She did. She rubbed them the way she did when she was alone. When she wasn't being a good girl at all. The more she played, the faster he teased her. She smiled. Immediate gratification. Yes.

"Take off your skirt."

She paused, opened her eyes to see him, and while their gazes locked, she unzipped the skirt. She thought he'd move his hand, but he didn't. She had no choice but to lift the skirt up all the way over her head. Then she let it drop.

She stood before him, in white satin panties and black high heels.

"You're exquisite," he whispered.

She lowered her gaze, suddenly shy.

"The most beautiful woman I've ever seen."

She didn't know how to respond, except to touch him. To show him that she wanted to see him, too.

He made her do all the work. She didn't mind. Not when he was making her feel so very good.

She got his belt open, then found his zipper. The pressure of his erection made things a bit tricky, but she managed. The whole time, he stared at her, thrumming with tension.

Slowly, because she wanted it to last and because he was making her clumsy and dizzy with the pressure of his finger, she lowered his pants until they dropped to pool at his feet. He wore black silk boxers that didn't do a thing to disguise his condition.

Even from this perspective, through his boxers, she could see he was magnificent. She hadn't realized when she'd seen him in the mirror. But he was... intimidating. Not enough to stop her, of course, but it did sober her a bit.

She rubbed him through the soft material, making him breath deeply. His control surprised her. He never stopped rubbing her, even when she hooked his waistband in her hands and eased the shorts down over his erection.

She froze when she saw him for the first time. Large, thick, hot. To have that inside her...

As if he'd read her mind, his finger moved farther back, then dipped inside.

She gasped with the intrusion, and he groaned as he thrust his finger in and in.

"Touch me," he said.

Her hand moved to his thick flesh. She wasn't sure what to do first, so she took his shaft in her hand.

As she explored him, he drew his wet finger from the lips between her legs and brought it up her belly leaving a long, musky, moist trail. He traced a line between her breasts to the hollow at the base of her throat, to her chin, her lower lip, and she took the finger into her mouth, tasting herself on his fingertip.

He jerked in her hand, and a drop of pearly liquid glistened at the tip. She wanted to taste him. Letting his finger go, she lowered herself until she rested on her knees, his erection right there. Leaning forward slowly, she touched her tongue to the bead, then closed her eyes. Bitter, salty, strange. The taste wasn't what she had expected.

She liked it. She liked that it wasn't sweet or bland, that it was like no other taste. She liked that she'd remember it forever.

"I can't…"

She looked up. "You can't what?"

"Stand it."

"What do you want?"

"You."

"Then, take me."

He cursed, grabbed her by the arms and pulled her to her feet, braced her against the wall. He kissed her relentlessly while he took hold of her legs. Lifting her as if she weighed nothing, he brought her off her feet, her legs around his waist.

She cried out even before he entered her. She could feel him tremble as he controlled his movements, and even though she was afraid it would hurt, she didn't want him controlled. She broke away from his kiss. "Don't be nice," she whispered again, making him understand.

He thrust inside her, all the way, filling her with his heat. It did hurt, but only for a moment. Then there was nothing but hot...hard...him deep inside, part of her flesh, part of her soul.

He kissed her again, as roughly as he thrust into her, and it was everything she'd dreamed, only more, impossibly more because it was *him* and...

She loved him.

Oh God. She clutched his back, held on to his hips, rode him, milked him, wept with the power of her feelings, at the depth of her need, and she loved him.

He touched her so deeply, and not simply with his cock. He touched her heart, he had changed her forever. Her eyes closed as he grew inside her, as she tightened around him.

His body held her against the wall, his gaze never wavering. He thrust again and again, teeth bared, breath straining.

She didn't recognize the onset of her orgasm. It wasn't like the others, when it was her own hand or her vibrator. This was like a tidal wave, a *tsunami,* swallowing her whole, spinning her, drowning her, and she must have screamed because she heard her voice from afar.

He pinned her against the wall, and his cry melted into hers as they came like thunder and lightning.

A long time later, he slid out of her, and her legs touched the earth.

Breathless, dizzy, still shivering, he led her past the couch to his bedroom. Tossing back the sheets, he waited until she lay down, then he crawled in next to her, brought the covers up and pulled her close.

Her eyes fluttered closed, and with her head cradled on his chest, she sighed, abandoning herself to sleep. In her dream, he said, ''I love you.''

16

JAY DIDN'T SLEEP, although, Christ, she'd wrung him out. Tonight hadn't gone the way he'd thought it would. Not by a long shot. The first time they'd made love had been raw, hungry, physical. The second time, once they had gotten to his bed, had been more tender, a gentle exploration. By the third time he'd come with her, he knew he was in deep trouble.

How had his plan gone so wrong? This was supposed to have been a diversion. Pleasant, yes, but nothing more. It was supposed to have been just sex.

So why was it that when he'd finally reached his goal, everything had fallen apart?

She sighed, moved her hand on his chest. He touched her hair, careful not to wake her. She'd curled into him, so trusting and at ease that she'd conked out before he'd turned off the light.

He'd wanted to free her of her inhibitions. To give her the confidence to let her wild side come out. Getting involved hadn't been an option.

Somewhere along the way, the power had shifted. He hadn't gotten it until tonight. Until he realized he wanted her beyond anything he'd ever wanted in his life. He needed her, and it scared the hell out of him.

The trip to Connecticut had been a bust, too. He'd delivered the bike, but he might as well have shipped it. The road, where he'd always found peace, had given him nothing. Confusion about his life, about Amelia, about his father. Wasn't it just a few weeks ago that his life had been completely together?

Dammit, he'd promised not to hurt her. She was a great lady and she deserved someone who could be a good husband, give her the white picket fence and all that bull. A guy like one of his brothers. They were marriage material, not him. Besides, there was a veritable smorgasbord of beautiful women all around him. Granted, Amelia was special. Extraordinary. But there were a lot of dishes out there he'd never tried.

So what if he couldn't imagine himself with anyone else? Tomorrow was another day, and when he'd cut it off with Amelia, he'd feel differently.

Shit. He hadn't meant for things to get this far out of hand. If he'd thought with his head instead of his cock, this wouldn't have happened at all. It was too late, now. She had feelings for him. Strong feelings. And no matter how he broke up with her, she was going to be crushed.

Maybe he should tell her about reading her journal. She'd be furious, and that would be the end of that. No. It would be easier for him, but she might misinterpret his intentions and go into hiding again. No matter what, he had to leave her her dignity.

He wouldn't call her again, that's all. She'd be sad, sure, so would he. But it would pass, and now that she was looking so hot, she'd meet other guys.

The thought didn't sit well. Amelia with another man? He thought of how he had wanted to hurt that guy at the frat party, and that was before…

Jay bit back a moan. He was so full of himself. He didn't want her to see anyone else. But he didn't want to commit, either. Maybe she'd be okay with that and he was worrying for nothing.

Yeah, right.

Man, he'd really screwed up this time. His father was right. He was a jerk. A selfish prick. Amelia deserved so much better.

Okay, so he wasn't going to call her. That's all. If…no, *when* she met someone else, he'd deal with it. He'd give her his blessing, unless the guy was a total jackass or something. But it would work out. He honestly wanted the best for her.

He petted her again, and she stirred. He pulled his hand back and got real quiet, but it was too late. Her head came up, and she smiled.

"Hi."

"Hi."

"What time is it?"

"About twelve."

"At night?"

"Yeah."

"Wow." She let her head fall on his chest. "I thought only guys went to sleep right after sex."

He chuckled. How could he not see her again?

"Did we eat dinner?"

"Nope. And I have a feeling we don't want to eat it now. It's chicken jerky."

"Oh."

"I can put something together."

"No, it's okay."

"Amelia, you have to be starving."

Her hand clasped his penis, and he nearly leapt out of the bed.

She just giggled. "I want fourths."

Jay couldn't hold back a whimper. This was not good. He'd have to be some kind of cad to make love to her now. Not when he knew it had to end. Still, the temptation was so damn great...

"What's wrong?"

"Uh...nothing."

"Jay?" She looked up at him, and he could see her confusion even in the dim light of the moon.

"I'm fine," he said. "I just thought we could, you know, cuddle for a bit, and then maybe go grab something to eat."

"Cuddle?"

He nodded. Smiled. The last thing on earth he wanted to do was cuddle, but he'd be damned if he let her know that.

"Hmm. Okay."

She relaxed again, but she didn't let go of him. Maybe she thought cuddling was something else. Regardless, he'd never survive. He was already half hard, and she'd touched him for—what, ten seconds?

"Amelia?"

"Yeah?"

"Honey, I have to get up."

"Why?"

"Bathroom."

Her hand disappeared. "Sorry."

"It's okay. You just rest. I'll be right out."

She yawned loudly. "Okay."

By the time he got to his feet, she'd wrapped her arms around his pillow and closed her eyes.

If he could stay in the bathroom long enough, she'd fall asleep. It was his only chance. Not that he didn't want to... No. For once in his life, he was going to do the right thing. He wasn't going to take advantage of her. Even though they'd already—

He closed the bathroom door as quietly as he could. Looking down, his predicament was painfully obvious. There was no way he could go back out there in this condition. Even if she was sleeping, she might wake up, and then he'd be trapped.

He took hold of his cock. It wouldn't take long. Knowing Amelia was out there right now, naked in his bed, was enough to make him lose it. He closed his eyes, leaned against the counter and remembered.

Nothing had ever felt as good as being inside her. He couldn't even explain why. Maybe because he understood her so well. Because he knew how much it had taken for her to be so outspoken, so overtly sexual. He'd seen the real Amelia, and no one else had. She'd given him a gift. The best gift he could give her in return was to leave her the hell alone.

He struggled back to the good memories, the feel of entering her for the first time. The sound of her whisper when she told him not to be nice. Shit, what irony.

Touching her, feeling her ride him, oh God, he was getting close and he had to bite his lip to stop from groaning. The torture of knowing she was so near made him insane. What had she done to him? What was he going to do?

AMELIA WOKE UP to sunlight. And an empty bed. She looked at the bedside clock. Seven-ten. Where was Jay?

She sat up and stretched, but her yawn cut off when she realized she'd fallen asleep last night. Okay, so they hadn't been doing it at the time, but still. She'd fallen asleep after teasing him. All he'd had to do was go to the bathroom. She'd never heard him come out.

She would make it up to him. She didn't want him thinking she didn't care. That she didn't want him. That was the farthest thing from the truth.

Last night had made things very clear. On her part, at least. She loved him deeply, and she wanted nothing more than to be with him. Although it scared her to death, she was going to tell him.

He might get freaked out, but something told her he wouldn't. The way he'd looked at her... It was as if she could see her own feelings in his eyes.

She slipped out of bed, stopped when she saw her clothes neatly folded on his chair. Sweet. She grabbed the bundle and headed for the bathroom, anxious to see him. Wondering if perhaps she shouldn't put on her clothes just yet.

She closed the bathroom door, and saw the note taped to the mirror.

Dear Amelia, I had to leave, I'm sorry. I didn't
want to wake you. There's orange juice and coffee in the kitchen, and the bagels are fresh. I'll
never forget last night.

It wasn't signed. She wondered about that briefly,
but it was probably nothing. He'd never forget last
night. Neither would she.

She wished he had gotten her up. She'd rather be
with him than sleep. Or almost anything else. Maybe
he'd like to come over tonight. She'd cook dinner,
and they'd actually eat it. She grinned. If she could
get rid of the roommates. Tabby would help with that.

She turned on the shower, and as it warmed, she
looked at the counter. His things. A razor and shaving
cream, menthol. His horsehair brush. She picked up
his bottle of cologne, Hugo Boss, and sniffed. She
shivered as his scent filled her.

Shaking her head, she put down the bottle, but she
didn't get in the shower just yet. She opened her
purse, got out her lipstick, Femme Fatale Red, and
wrote him a note on the mirror.

She chuckled all through her shower. Today was
going to be a good day.

JAY HUNG UP the phone. Brian had called to report an
Amelia sighting at the café. But Jay wouldn't see her.
It was the right thing to do, but he felt like shit. Which
was probably just what he deserved. Leaving her this
morning, knowing he wouldn't get to call her or talk
to her, had made him sick.

He leaned back in his chair, stared at his computer screen. The temptation to log onto TrueConfessions.com had him by the short hairs—but he wouldn't. Although, now that he wasn't going to see her—

He stood up so quickly his chair smashed into the wall behind him. This was ridiculous. He felt like a teenager mooning over the prom queen. Even when he'd been a teenager he'd never felt like this.

Since the time he'd first become interested in the opposite sex, the game had always been in his court. He'd set the ground rules, and if things got sticky, he moved on. The system worked. He never lacked for companionship in or out of bed, and he liked to think his lady friends got as much out of their time together as he did. Uncomplicated, straightforward, he'd assumed it would go on like that forever.

But even if he did consider, for a moment, the possibility of settling down, he couldn't do it with Amelia. He'd have to tell her about reading her journal, and then she'd hate him, and that would be that. They wouldn't be together, and she'd probably revert back to her old self, which would kill him. The only good thing to come out of this fiasco was her belief in herself, and *that* he wouldn't take away for the world.

The more he thought about what she'd done, how she'd faced her fears, the worse he felt about what *he'd* done. Only, if he hadn't set things in motion, she wouldn't have changed. It was a no-win situation, and the best thing he could do was step back, close the door and forget about it.

As if that were possible.

Forgetting Amelia wasn't going to be easy. Maybe it wasn't supposed to be easy.

AMELIA DUCKED BEHIND her textbook, but she wasn't quick enough. Tabby came into her room and sat on the edge of her bed.

"What's wrong?"

Amelia sniffed as she dabbed tears with her tissue. "I don't know."

Tabby quirked her eyebrow. "Right. You're crying because *Medical Ethics in America* is a moving, emotional read."

Amelia smiled, although the last thing on earth she felt was happy. "It's been four days."

"Since?"

"Jay called."

"Four days isn't that long."

"Five days ago, we slept together."

Tabby blinked. "You did?"

"Don't sound so shocked. I'm not a nun."

"I know, it's just that... Never mind. He hasn't called you since you had sex?"

Amelia shook her head, fresh tears clouding her vision. "I screwed up, but I don't know how. He didn't even wait for me the next morning. All I got was a note."

Tabby pushed Amelia's feet aside and sat back on the bed, legs crossed, clearly settling in for a long chat. "First of all, you didn't screw up."

"How do you know?"

"Because I know you. Listen, kiddo, I know more about these things than you, and I promise, you didn't mess up."

"Then, why hasn't he called?"

"There could be lots of reasons. All having to do with him. Not you."

"Like?"

"He could have someone else in his life."

"I don't think so."

"But you don't know for sure."

Amelia nodded. She put her book on her lap and grabbed another tissue. In her old life, she would have been sleeping by now. She didn't stay up past midnight, unless there was some kind of emergency. Since Jay, that had changed, too. She'd been up later, done less studying. Her whole routine had been shaken up.

"You know what I think it is?"

"What?"

"I think he got scared."

"Of what? I wasn't going to hurt him."

Tabby tried unsuccessfully to hide a grin. "I meant that he might be afraid of his feelings for you."

"What does that mean?"

"From what you've told me about Jay, he isn't a one-woman kind of guy. Which means he knows how to keep an emotional distance. And if you threatened that—"

"How? I didn't ask him to marry me or even go steady."

"Go steady? Honey, you have got to stop watching those Gidget movies."

"Tabby."

"Okay. Sheesh. I'm talking about him being scared of his own feelings. Men are like that. At least, most men. They feel vulnerable when they care. It makes certain guys feel out of control."

"Well, I can't help that."

"Which is exactly what I'm saying. It's more than likely he hasn't called because he's going through his own changes. So give him a break."

Amelia blew her nose, then adjusted the pillow behind her back. She was in her flannel pj's—ugly, practical, old. She felt as though they didn't belong to her anymore.

"You know," she said, "I figured you would have told me to forget about him."

"Nope. Not this guy."

"Why?"

Tabby smiled warmly. "Look at you. Whatever his sins are, they can't take away from the fact that he turned your life around. I never thought I'd see you like this. Confident, playing up your looks, and you're not blushing all the time. Hey, I don't know if you two are going to live happily ever after, but damn, girl. Be grateful. No matter what, you're ready to face life in a whole new way."

"I suppose."

"I know it sucks. But give it time. Let him come

to his own conclusions. Remember, it ain't over till it's over."

"How come you're so smart?"

Tabby laughed. "Because it's your life. I'm a complete moron about my own."

"You are not."

She climbed off the bed, stretched her arms over her head, then laid her palms on the floor. Bent double, she looked at Amelia. "It's always easier to see everyone else's life with clarity. But when it's us, we have all our fears getting in the way."

"It's true. It is about fear. Tabby, I don't want to lose him. He's the best thing that's ever happened to me."

Tabby stood. "Honey, he's the only thing that's ever happened to you."

"Which doesn't mean he isn't the right guy for me."

"True. Look, if he doesn't call tomorrow, call him."

"I couldn't."

"Why not?"

"Because."

"Good answer."

Amelia rolled her eyes. "Because I don't know if he wants to see me again. If he doesn't, I'll be humiliated."

"You'll be humiliated, anyway, so what's the problem?"

"Gee, thanks. You've made me feel so much better."

"I know. It's a gift." Tabby stood up straight and grinned. "Go to sleep. Things will be clearer tomorrow."

"Promise?"

"Yes. I'll even write it down if you want." Tabby walked to the door, then stopped short and spun around. "You slept with him."

Amelia felt her face heat. She nodded, suddenly bashful.

"How could you let me walk out this door without details?"

"I'm not going to describe what happened. It's personal."

"Screw personal. I want to hear everything." She came back in the room, but instead of getting on the bed, she climbed up on the small desk.

"I can't say."

"Jeez, Amelia, I tell you everything."

"You do not."

"But that's only because you don't ask."

She had to laugh at that. Tabby's logic was nothing if not consistent. "Okay. I'm not divulging everything. But I will tell you one thing. It's uncanny. If it hadn't happened to me, I wouldn't have believed it."

"What?"

"He can read me. I can't explain it better than that. He just knows things about me he couldn't possibly know. When we made love, it was right out of my fantasies. But it's been like that from the first day."

"Maybe he's your soul mate."

"I think so. I hope so. God, Tabby, if I lose him—"

"Stop. Right there. You don't know what's going to happen, so why focus on the negative. Let it go. Trust it'll turn out the way it's supposed to."

"Tabby, I love him. I do. With all my heart. He's the one, I'd bet my life on it."

"Then, he'll call." Tabby jumped down from the desk, kissed Amelia on the forehead, and headed out the door. "Now go to sleep," she said over her shoulder.

"Yes, ma'am."

When she was alone again, Amelia tried to read her textbook, but it was no good. She couldn't think of anything but Jay. Maybe he'd call tomorrow. And if he didn't, then she'd call him.

He was worth it. They were worth it.

17

JAY PICKED UP THE PHONE, dialed five numbers, then hung up again. It had been six days since he'd last seen Amelia, and things had gone progressively downhill.

She was constantly on his mind. She'd been in his dreams. Several times, he'd justified calling her, rationalized reading her journal—only to find he couldn't go through with it. Hell of a time to develop a conscience.

He wished he'd stayed at work. Karl had been avoiding him, with good cause. He'd been a card-carrying bastard, taking his unhappiness out on everyone around him. Today, Karl had told him straight out to call Amelia and quit being such an idiot.

Jay got up, walked into the kitchen, looked in the fridge. Nothing had changed since the last time he'd looked inside, which was—what, a half hour ago? Chinese food cartons, one with chopsticks still in it. Two pieces of dead pizza, jelly, beer, OJ and milk. He closed the door, debating whether he should go out to eat, call in take-out, or just forget about the whole business. He wasn't hungry, just bored.

He wanted to call Amelia.

Shit.

He wandered back into the living room and sat at his computer. He'd do a little surfing, maybe go to a chat room or something. He logged on and did a quick survey of his e-mail. Nothing interesting. Then he clicked on his Favorite Places. Of course, the first thing he saw was TrueConfessions.com. Before he could change his mind, he went there.

If he read her stuff now, he'd know he was irredeemable. A jackass of the first order. So why was he torturing himself?

Troubled? Confession Helps! Totally Private, Completely Anonymous. Say Anything.

He read the words over and over, and then he was on a blank page, a confession page of his own, and his fingers flew on the keyboard as he poured out his soul.

It never occurred to me that I could hurt her like this. That I could hurt like this. It all went south, and I'm not sure when, or how. I just know I don't deserve her, and that I miss her badly, and fuck it, I think I'm in love with her. I don't know what to do. Who to blame, except myself.

I don't know that I can hold off calling her for much longer. I feel like a junkie going cold turkey, and I'm not strong enough. I need her like air, like water. I want to make love to her, and I want everything to be fine. I want it to be like it was.

He stopped, hardly believing he'd said so much. He barely recognized himself. As he scanned the frenzied words, his gut clenched and he almost put his fist through the monitor.

He picked up the phone and dialed Amelia's number. She answered on the second ring.

She was more nervous than the first time she'd stood in front of his door. Nervous and excited, and she wished he would hurry up because her heart was about to beat out of her chest.

When he'd called, she nearly wept. He said he'd explain when she got to his place. He said it would be okay. He said he'd missed her.

The door opened, and seeing him was like a reprieve. As if she'd been pardoned by the governor, saved from a slow, aching death.

He looked at her with a wild hunger as he pulled her into his arms. For a moment he just looked at her, and there was such longing in his gaze that she felt foolish for doubting him.

"Baby," he whispered, "I've missed you."

"Me, too. So much."

Her eyes fluttered closed as he kissed her, a long deep passionate kiss that melted her very bones. His hands on her back clutched tightly, as if he never wanted to let her go.

It was she who pulled back first. Not because she wanted to, but because the door was still open and she'd heard footsteps. She was braver now, sure, but not an exhibitionist.

He kicked the door closed with his foot, crooked his arm around her neck and pulled her tight. His erection against her hip was hot, thick, aching. She moaned as she ran her hand down his body until she touched him, cupped his shaft and squeezed him gently.

He bucked against her, his head snapping back as if he'd been shocked. "Babe, you can't do that. Not if you want me to survive."

"What if I don't?" she whispered. "What if I want to make love to you until there's nothing left?"

He looked into her eyes, searching for something—she wasn't sure what. "I'd do that for you."

She believed him. As poetic as it sounded, she knew he would go to the ends of the earth for her, take a bullet, swim the ocean. It was all there, right in the depth of his eyes. But there was also a sadness there she didn't remember. That made her insides ache.

"Come," he said, slipping his hands down her arms. "I've got wine."

She followed him into the kitchen. He poured her a glass of Merlot, and took a drink of his own. "Are you hungry?"

"No. I ate before I came."

"Smart girl."

"Why did you call, Jay? What is it you want to tell me?"

He took in a great breath and let it out slowly. She couldn't read him, at least not his eyes. His body, beautiful in worn jeans and a flannel shirt, seemed tense. Shoeless again, the toes on his right foot curled in his white sock.

"I missed you," he said finally. "More than I wanted to."

She closed her eyes. "I don't know what that means."

She heard the *clink* of his glass on the counter, then his hands grasped her shoulders. "I can't get you out of my head. Not even when I sleep. You're in my dreams, in my thoughts. I keep thinking I see you out of the corner of my eye, but it's not you. I just want it to be you."

Her blood flowed and her heart beat, and she stood up on her toes until her lips touched his. With a groan, he kissed her once more, and it was familiar and thrilling—the same kiss, the kiss that would go on forever.

They touched each other all over. Both of them anxious, needy, hungry, until it wasn't possible to stand another second. He pulled away, his lips moist and perfect. "I want to make love with you," he whispered. "I need to make love with you."

She nodded, and he sighed, and they walked somehow all the way across the apartment until they were in his room. She started to take off her shirt, but his hands stopped her.

He took hold of the bottom of the angora sweater and pulled it up slowly, revealing her bra, her neck, and then up her arms and off. He bent his head and kissed the tops of her breasts, his hair tickling her chin.

Then his fingers found the row of buttons on her jeans, and with surprising dexterity, undid them. He hooked his thumbs on her waistband, and lowered himself along with her jeans and panties. He kissed her tummy on the way down. His hot breath at the juncture of her thighs made her shiver. She put her hands on his shoulders to step out of her clothes, and then he took off her shoes and socks, slowly, reverently, until she was naked before him.

He kissed her all the way up—hot lips on her calf, her thigh, the hollow at her hipbone. He lingered at her breasts, unclasping her bra, then kissing, licking, sucking until she moaned and grasped his hair, guiding him to her nipple.

She trembled as he suckled, but she wanted more. She wanted him naked, and she wanted to feel his skin on her skin, his body in her body.

"Jay," she whispered.

He stopped, not releasing her from his lips.

"Please, let me undress you."

He lapped her nipple one last time before he stood. She shook off her bra, and didn't care where it fell because she was already undoing the buttons of his shirt. With trembling fingers, she got to the last one, then pushed the shirt open. His chest, with a smattering of dark hair, seemed impossibly beautiful, and she kissed him all over, everywhere she could reach, while she undid his jeans.

As she eased the zipper down, her hand once again

brushed his hard length, and his sharp intake of breath made her very careful not to touch it again. Yet.

She pulled down his pants, releasing him from the constraint of the denim and his underwear, and his penis stood up so hard and fine that it brushed his stomach, right under his belly button. She bent over and ran her tongue up the backside, tracing the veins, remembering his taste and his scent.

He groaned and pulled her up, and after he stepped out of his clothes, he brought her close. Her body and his touched from shoulder to knee, and the warmth was overshadowed by the banked energy. She felt as if they could light up Manhattan.

"Bed," he whispered.

She walked with him, unwilling to let go completely. She needed to touch him—the more, the better. When they reached the bed he threw back the comforter and pulled her down underneath him.

Then they were kissing, as if they'd never kissed, as if they'd always kissed. His hot tongue thrusting, making her his own. She rubbed herself against him wantonly, loving the feel of his cock, knowing soon it would be intimately part of her.

Jay's hand slid down her side, then slipped to the lips of her sex. She gasped as his finger entered her.

"So wet," he said, his lips brushing hers, his breath mingling with her own. "So beautiful. I can't stand it. I have to—"

She spread her legs in invitation, and a moment later he entered her, slowly, inch by inch, until he filled her. She wrapped her legs around his back, her arms around his neck.

She opened her eyes to stare into his, and heartbeat after heartbeat, neither of them moved. Her muscles contracted around him, and she felt him pulse inside her, but the real heat was in his gaze.

"I love you," she said. "When you didn't call, I nearly went insane. You're everything I've ever wanted, ever dreamed of. I never knew I could feel this way."

He closed his eyes, but only for a moment. When he opened them again, he locked on to her gaze once more. "I love you," he said. "It wasn't in my plans. I didn't know I was going to fall, but I did. Oh God."

He moved inside her, pulling out until only the head was still between her lips, then he thrust back inside. "Mine," he whispered. "Mine." And then he couldn't talk.

At the word, she felt the stirrings of her orgasm, and she clung to him as he branded her, as he melted into her. His hips moved faster, and the heat built to an unbearable pitch. She gasped at the first wave of her climax, and tightened her muscles, squeezing him—and that's all it took. His head went back, he pushed inside her as deeply as he could go, and then he poured himself into her.

She trembled, tensed, came so deeply that it was from her soul, but she needed more. She took his face between her hands, brought his gaze back to hers. "Yours," she said. "I'm yours."

JAY KISSED HER until he couldn't breathe. Until he'd grown soft, and his arms couldn't hold him up anymore. Reluctantly, he slipped out of her and rolled to her side. It was a struggle, but he found the comforter and covered them both. Then he wrapped her in his arms and legs, his head and hers on the same pillow.

"I was so afraid," she said, her voice so soft that he had to strain to hear her. "I thought I'd lost you."

"Amelia—"

She touched his lips. "Wait, please."

He nodded, grateful for the reprieve. The truth was, he still didn't know what to do. He didn't want to come clean, for his own sake as much as hers. But how could they move forward with this between them?

He wanted to move forward. When he'd opened that door and pulled her into his arms, all his doubts had vanished. He was in love for the first time in his life. For the only time. She'd breached his defenses, knocked down his walls, and he needed her.

He wanted to spend the rest of his life with her, but he knew without a doubt that it would fall apart if he didn't confess. He would. But not here. Not yet. He didn't want to ruin this.

Her hand glided over his chest. "I think I knew this was going to happen from the very first time you talked to me. Do you remember? In the café. You gave me a pen."

"I remember."

"You made me blush."

"That wasn't very difficult."

She grinned. "No, it wasn't." She kissed his chin. "I'm so grateful you saw me. That you took the time to look. No one ever had. I was lost before you. I've never experienced anything like it. You know me so well, better than I know myself."

"You're the one who did the changing. Not me. I don't want you to forget that."

"I won't. I promise."

They lapsed into a comfortable silence, and Jay memorized the feel of her. He rubbed her tummy in slow circles, sniffed her hair, got as close as he could. He had no idea if they could weather the coming storm. He hoped so.

"I'm going back to school," he said. "I'm going for my Master's degree in Literature."

She smiled. "Oh, honey. That's wonderful. I'm so glad for you. Hey, maybe we'll have some classes together. Wouldn't that be a kick?"

"Are you majoring in Lit?"

She shook her head. "No. Ethics."

Ethics. Jesus, that was just perfect. He smiled as the last few shards of his world crumbled around him.

AMELIA DIDN'T WANT TO MOVE. She'd never felt safer or more loved in her life. She'd never belonged anywhere as she did in Jay's arms. But she had to get something to drink. An hour ago it had been a passing thought. Now, she was pretty much desperate.

"Honey?" she whispered, not sure if Jay was awake. His eyes had been closed for a while.

"Yeah?"

"I'm going to get some water. Do you want anything?"

He rolled to his back. "I'll go."

"You will not. Just stay put. I'll be back in a second." She got out of bed, surprised at the chill. The closest thing to a robe was Jay's flannel shirt, which she put on before she padded out to the living room. She hurried, anxious to get back to bed. In her haste, she banged the hell out of her shin on the corner of his desk. Grimacing, she bent down to rub the spot and saw a piece of paper lying just under the desk. She pulled it out, and put it on his keyboard. She hobbled a few steps, then stopped and went back to look at the paper again.

She read the first few lines, and her blood went cold. She knew the words. She'd written them. It was a page from her journal. From the *anonymous* journal that she'd kept at TrueConfessions.com. How?

She read the whole thing through, telling herself this wasn't really happening. It was a dream. A nightmare. She'd fallen asleep and…

Oh God.

She read on, trying not to panic, trying to think of some other explanation, any other explanation. But these were her words. Her fantasy. A private, intimate admission. She could hardly breathe as she realized what this meant. He'd read her journal. For how long? From the beginning? Is that why…? No wonder he knew so much about her. It couldn't be. Jay wouldn't.

They'd just made love. He'd looked at her with such tenderness.

And yet, in a chilling way, it made so much sense. She'd been an idiot not to see it before. Her gaze went back to the page. There was no mistake. No mix-up. Jay had seduced her using her stolen diary.

She clutched his shirt closed as she struggled for control. It was like being in an earthquake. The very ground beneath her feet had shifted. Everything she'd believed about him was a lie.

Tears blinded her for a moment, and her heart beat so hard she thought she might die. She *wanted* to die. How could he have done that? How could he have made her think—

She had to get out. She couldn't even bear to look at him. Humiliation like she'd never known before flooded her, making it hard to think, to move.

What an incredible fool she was. Naive, stupid, the perfect target for a con man like Jay. She'd believed him, believed *in him*. She'd loved him with all her heart.

She was seconds away from losing it, big time. She turned, went back to the bedroom, grabbed her clothes from the floor, and made it to the bathroom without throwing up.

Shaking violently, she somehow got dressed. Praying he was asleep, she opened the door a crack. His eyes were closed. It killed her to look at him. To know it was all a joke, a game, at her expense. The bastard. How could she possibly still want him?

She'd figure that out later. For now, she had to

escape. Moving as quietly as she could, she walked through the bedroom, got her jacket and her purse, and then she scurried to the living room, closing the door quietly behind her.

Standing in the deserted hallway, she couldn't fight the tears any longer. With great sobbing gasps she stumbled to the elevator and pressed the button, afraid he'd notice she was gone and come after her.

The elevator door opened quickly and she rushed inside, blindly pushing the buttons on the console. The doors closed, and she cried so hard she fell against the wall. Her legs lost their strength and she slid down to the floor. She huddled there, her heart shattering and shattering as the elevator came to a stop. She would have stayed there forever if she could have. But she had to get out, get home.

She struggled to her feet, wiped her eyes with the arm of her jacket and headed for the street. For a cab that would take her away. Away from him.

18

JAY WOKE to an empty bed. He glanced at the clock, surprised that it was past one. His hand moved over the space next to him, but there was no warmth. His gut tightened as he threw back the covers and headed across the room. Her clothes weren't on the floor. She wasn't in the bathroom.

After a quick minute to take care of business, he pulled on his jeans and went to the living room, already knowing he wouldn't find her there. Something had happened, something to make her leave. But what?

He saw a sheet of paper on his keyboard. A note? He picked it up, and as he read it the life drained out of him. It wasn't a note. It was a page from her journal. He'd thought he'd gotten rid of everything, but somehow he'd missed this.

Shit. Dammit to hell. He should have told her. If he hadn't been such a coward, he would have faced the music and tried to make it easier for her.

He'd just wanted to make love to her once before he confessed. Like everything else concerning Amelia, he'd screwed this up, too.

He crumpled the paper and threw it in the trash.

He needed to talk to her. To explain. He wondered if she'd listen.

If the roles were reversed, he wouldn't. He would tell her to go to hell.

Numb, he sank to the edge of the couch and cradled his face in his hands. This was worse than he'd ever imagined. Infinitely worse. He'd never felt so goddamn alone in his life.

AMELIA STARED at her calendar, hardly believing her eyes. It was a month and two days since that night at Jay's. A month and two days of hell.

He'd called her and called her, until Donna had told him flat out not to call again. He'd written letter after letter, which she'd trashed without opening. He'd come to the apartment twice.

Finally, last week, his efforts had stopped. She'd gotten her point across. She'd been strong and stayed strong. So, why did it still hurt so bad?

She thought about him constantly. Had forgotten what it felt like to be happy. At first, she'd wanted to crawl back in her cave, but she couldn't even do that. There was no comfort in hiding, no solace in invisibility. She'd changed, and for better or worse, the change was permanent.

Rather than fight it, she made it her focus. Five days after that night, she'd quit her job at the library and found a new one as a waitress at a local coffee shop. Her income went up, and with the extra money she'd added to her wardrobe. She'd studied, but not obsessively, and was thankful her grades hadn't suffered.

Several people in her life, starting with the roommates, had commented on her strength, her determination. Kathy couldn't believe her quick recovery, and Donna had actually said she'd like to be like Amelia. It should have felt wonderful. But nothing felt wonderful.

It was all an act. Inside, she felt crippled, broken. Her heart continued to beat, her lungs continued to breathe, her eyes continued to see, but it was all mechanical, rote. She wasn't there. She never seemed to be anywhere but in a strange, painful limbo.

Despite everything, knowing all she did, she couldn't escape the fact that she still loved him. Only, she didn't write about it anymore. No more journal, no more cyber café. No more trust. Just emptiness. Longing. Sadness as deep as the ocean.

A tap at her bedroom door pulled her out of her reverie. It was Donna.

"You don't have to knock."

"I know. I just didn't want to scare you."

"Thanks."

The blonde entered the room, but there was something odd about her. Something she was hiding behind her back.

"What's going on?"

Donna smiled nervously. "Well, I did something."

"What?"

"Something you may want to shoot me for."

Amelia stood up, panic filling her chest. She couldn't handle another betrayal. She'd never survive it. "What did you do?"

Donna brought her hand out from behind her back. She held a stack of letters. "I kept these."

Amelia knew they were Jay's letters, and she resented the surge of hope that swelled in her chest. How could there be hope? There was no excuse for what he did. None in the world.

"I don't want them."

"Are you sure?"

Amelia nodded.

"Okay, if you really don't, I'll throw them away. But, Amelia..."

Donna blushed, which wasn't at all like her. Something else was going on here. Amelia sat down on her bed, and Donna joined her, still holding the letters.

"Go on," Amelia said. "Spit it out."

"Okay, but this isn't easy for me. I mean, it's not as if I'm any good at relationships or anything. I have no business telling you this."

"Telling me what?"

Donna exhaled. "I think what he did was wrong. But not fatally wrong."

"What do you mean?"

"He shouldn't have looked at your journal, but I don't believe he was playing you for a fool. I think he fell in love with you, just like you fell in love with him."

"Donna, what happened? Why are you saying this?"

"I saw him. Two days ago. He was at that cyber café you like so much. I went there with this guy I know from class, and, anyway, Jay was there and he didn't see me. Amelia, he looked so miserable. Not sick or anything, but all the stuff that was so incredibly hot about him, I don't know, faded. I ended up talking to this guy Brian. When I told him who I was, he asked me to ask you to please reconsider. He didn't know what had happened, and Jay won't talk about it, but Brian hadn't ever seen him like that."

"Whatever he's going through is his own fault. He brought this on himself."

"I know." Donna pursed her lips for a moment. "I just have one question for you, and then I'll drop it."

"What?"

"Why did you write your journal online if you didn't want anyone to read it?"

JAY FINISHED READING the letter from the admissions office at NYU. He'd been accepted for the program without much fuss; they'd gotten his transcripts from Cornell and that had paved the way. He'd be starting next semester.

The temptation was to toss the letter, to forget about school. But he wasn't going to do that. Whatever else had happened during his time with Amelia, he'd made some decisions about his life that he wouldn't abandon. He'd watched her face her fears, look at who she really was, and she'd stepped out on that fragile limb of change. How could he do less?

It didn't matter a damn what his father thought of him. Jay had to make his decisions about his future for himself. When he wasn't thinking about Amelia, his focus went to this dilemma. After all the excuses and reasons, it came down to some very simple truths. He missed writing. He wanted to do it again, even though he wasn't sure he could. He loved the shop but it wasn't the answer. At least, not the only answer.

He didn't know if he'd end up teaching, or what. It didn't matter. As long as he was taking one step at a time, being honest with himself, and open to the experience, he couldn't lose. If it meant his father accepted him, great. If not, he'd live.

That's the thing. He'd live. After losing Amelia, it hadn't seemed possible, but the days kept passing and he just kept on. He missed her like hell. Yet he sold bikes, shot pool, read the paper.

Always, she was there, in the quiet moments, in an unexpected sound. She was there, and it didn't seem likely she'd ever go away.

AT TWO-TWENTY in the morning, Amelia opened the first letter. She sat curled up in the big living room chair, a cup of peppermint tea on the table beside her. The others were asleep, and the city was oddly quiet.

Her fingers shook as she pulled the letter out of the envelope. She started crying before reading the first word.

Dear Amelia,

I'm sorry. I know that's pitiful, and it doesn't mean anything but it's true. I'm sorry that I was a fool, that I took advantage of you, that I breached your privacy. But I also know I'm not sorry. Not sorry I met you, that I got to know you, that we spent time together.

I am in love with you. You probably won't believe it. I would gladly spend the rest of my life proving it to you. It's no justification, but I honestly didn't think I was doing anything wrong. Not at first, anyway. Even before I read your journal, I saw something in you. A spark hiding behind your blush. I wanted to know that Amelia. I wanted her to come out and play. I used the wrong means, but it would have been infinitely worse not to have known you at all.

You're the bravest, kindest, most loving person I've ever met, and when I'm with you, I want to be brave and kind and loving.

Maybe, someday, you'll find it in your heart to forgive me. When, if, you do, I'll be here.

I love you. Please believe that, if nothing else. I love you.

Jay

As tears rolled down her cheeks, she thought

about all that had happened. It had been a few weeks, that's all, and yet she'd become someone new. She'd blossomed like a rose from his tender care. She'd found what she'd been looking for, asking for, in her journal.

She'd once written that she wished someone would see her. Would see the truth of her behind her facade. And that's exactly what Jay had done.

Donna's words had haunted her all night. Why had she written her journal online? And why was she so hurt when all Jay had done was answer her prayers?

She folded the letter and reached for the next one. She read them all, most of them twice. And then she knew what she had to do.

JAY PUT DOWN HIS CUP, puzzled. Something had shifted. He'd be hard-pressed to say what. Electrical, somehow. As if lightning were going to strike.

He looked at Brian, but his friend was still glued to his computer. No one else in the café seemed to feel it. He kept expecting the sensation to pass, but it just got stronger.

The door opened, and he turned, but the glare from the sunlight blinded him momentarily. It wasn't until the door closed again that he saw her.

Amelia.

His heart thudded in his chest. Standing, he took a step toward her, then stopped. What if she didn't realize he was here? What if she saw him and bolted?

Not yet. He needed her to stay a little longer. He'd thought he memorized every detail about her, but now he saw how ludicrous that was. Her hair had more red in the soft waves. He'd gotten her skin tone all wrong, and her lips. How could he have forgotten the plush pink?

He knew her body as well as he'd ever known another human being, yet staring at her now he discovered her all over again. He ached for her like a starving man yearns for bread. He finally identified the shape of what was missing in him.

"Amelia."

Even though he'd whispered her name, she found him, met his gaze. A moment passed where he couldn't breathe, but then she headed toward him.

He cataloged every part of her. The coat, blue, one he'd never seen. Beneath that, just a strip visible, a green sweater to match her eyes. The jeans she'd worn that last night.

He waited until she'd come half the distance of the café, then he walked toward her, praying this was the miracle he'd never dared to hope for.

The closer he got, the more vulnerable she appeared. Clearly afraid, she didn't let it stop her. Not for a second. Then she was in front of him, an arm's length away. For a long time, they stared into each other's eyes, remembering. He wanted her more than he could stand. He wanted to say the right thing, to get every nuance perfect so he wouldn't screw up again.

Her lips curved into a slight smile. "Hi."

"Hi."

"I thought we should talk."

He nodded.

"Want to go for a walk?"

He didn't trust himself to say any more. Instead, he headed for the door, and she fell in beside him. Having her this close made him crazy to touch her. To kiss her. But he hid it all. He had to know what she was going to say.

They stepped outside to the unseasonably warm November afternoon. The crisp, clean air shimmered with the low sun. There were people and cars and buses and signs, and he didn't see any of it. Only her.

She led him down the street, away from his shop, to Washington Square Park. Pigeons fled before their footsteps, and a man with long gray hair played classical guitar for dollar bills.

There was an empty bench away from most everyone, and that's where they sat. Her knee touched his.

"I've done a lot of thinking," she said. She pressed her lips together, looked at him, then away. But her gaze came back before she spoke again. "I don't like what you did. It wasn't fair. And it wasn't nice."

He nodded, his hopes sinking like lead weights in a pond. "I know that."

"I don't know what your motivation was, what you hoped to achieve. All I know for sure is what I was when I was with you. I changed. And not just outside. The clothes, the makeup, none of that matters. The important thing is that I stopped hiding. I came out of darkness, the lonely prison I'd built all by myself. You saw me. And because you saw me, I was able to see myself through different eyes."

He wanted to speak, but he waited. If he had to, he'd wait forever. Just to be near her.

"But I had to look at my part in this, too. I know enough about the Internet to understand that nothing is truly private. Especially at a site like True-Confessions.com. It's designed for peeking, for reading private thoughts. So why wouldn't you look? Granted, I'm still not sure how you figured out Good Girl was me, but it doesn't matter. I could have written a private journal, but I didn't. I wanted you to read about me. Not that I knew at the time it was going to be you, but Jay, you're exactly what I dreamed about.

"I'm not talking about the pen trick, or how you knew about the Guggenheim. It goes much deeper than that. You helped me see that I was worth fighting for. That I didn't have to hide. I fell in love with you because of who you are, not because you knew I wanted to ride on a Harley, but because every time you looked at me, I felt special. I felt needed, and wanted, and sexy and so much more. You were so easy to fall in love with."

She paused and took a deep breath. "I don't know what you want. And it scares the hell out of me to tell you what I want, but I'm going to. I'm going to put it all out there because with you, I can risk everything. And I can't expect to hear the truth from you if I'm not willing to speak it.''

He opened his mouth, but she shook her head.

"Not yet, please.''

He actually felt grateful that he didn't have to speak. He wasn't very sure of his voice.

"I want to get past this. I want to be with you. I want to love you. I want you to love me.''

That was it. There was no more. It was his turn.

AMELIA KEPT HER HANDS in her pockets, tightly fisted to stop the shaking. She'd done it. Said it all. And waiting for him to speak was torture.

But even if he passed, even if he laughed, she'd know she'd done her best. She'd know she could walk through fire. What an incredible gift.

He looked at her for a moment, then he sighed. "I don't understand what I could have done to deserve you.''

Tears filled her eyes and spilled down her cheeks, and there wasn't a thing she could do to stop them.

"I've had that same month to think," he said. "And I'm not all that sure I'm sorry. If that's what it took to be here, then I have no regrets. The only thing I would have changed is that I hurt you. I never want to do that again.''

He cleared his throat, searching for the right words. "You're not the only one who's changed. I've had to look, really look, at who I am and what I'm doing with my life. I've started writing again, and I owe that to you. I'm going back to school. I don't know what's going to come of any of it. I might fall flat on my face. But I'll have tried. You make me brave. And strong.

"I want to get past this. I want to be with you." He leaned forward and brushed her lips with his own. "I want to love you, Amelia. Forever."

He stood, and so did she, falling into his arms. He kissed her then, and because there were miracles, it was the same kiss, only now it was stronger, sweeter. He held her tight as the kiss went on and on. And the world outside their small circle disappeared.

Epilogue

Two years later...

AMELIA OPENED THE BOOK to the flyleaf. She read the dedication again, even though she'd read it a dozen times.

> To my beautiful bride, Amelia, for more than I can ever say. I love you.
> And to my father, for believing in me when I didn't believe in myself.

She handed the book to Jay, then turned to her father-in-law. "I'm glad you made it, Lucas."

"I wouldn't have missed it." He looked her over from head to toe. "I hope you're taking good care of my grandchild."

"I'm reading her Shakespeare every night."

"Hmm," Lucas said. "I understand Mozart is good, too."

She smiled and ran her hand over her belly. Four months along, and already huge. But she didn't mind. Not at all.

Jay signed the book for his father and handed it to him. "Thanks, Dad. For everything."

Lucas cleared his throat. "I'm proud of you."

Amelia studied her husband's expression. The reconciliation between father and son was too new to take for granted. But Jay smiled. Nodded.

She sighed, looking at the incredible turnout for the book signing. Jay had sworn no one would show up, but she'd known better. The reviews had been astounding, and he'd had an excerpt in the *New Yorker*.

None of that mattered nearly as much as the fact that Jay had done it. He'd struggled and fought and cursed and quit a hundred times, but in the end, he'd finished the book.

She'd never been so proud of anyone.

He touched her hand, and she turned to smile at him. "What?"

He shook his head without saying a word. But she knew exactly what he meant. She leaned over and kissed his cheek. He sighed.

It was perfect.

community | membership

buy books | authors | online reads | magazine | learn to write

Visit eHarlequin.com to discover your one-stop shop for romance:

buy books

- ♥ Choose from an extensive selection of Harlequin, Silhouette, MIRA and Steeple Hill books.

- ♥ Enjoy top Harlequin authors and *New York Times* bestselling authors in Other Romances: Nora Roberts, Jayne Ann Krentz, Danielle Steel and more!

- ♥ Check out our deal-of-the-week specially discounted books at up to 30% off!

- ♥ Save in our Bargain Outlet: hard-to-find books at great prices! Get 35% off your favorite books!

- ♥ Take advantage of our low-cost flat-rate shipping on all the books you want.

- ♥ Learn how to get FREE Internet-exclusive books.

- ♥ In our Authors area find the currently available titles of all the best writers.

- ♥ Get a sneak peek at the great reads for the next three months.

- ♥ Post your personal book recommendation online!

- ♥ Keep up with all your favorite miniseries.

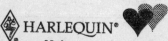

HARLEQUIN®

Makes any time special®—online...

Visit us at
www.eHarlequin.com

HINTBB

HARLEQUIN®
Temptation

It's hot...and it's out of control!

This spring, the forecast is hot and steamy!
Don't miss these bold, provocative, ultra-sexy books!

PRIVATE INVESTIGATIONS by Tori Carrington
April 2002
Secretary-turned-P.I. Ripley Logan never thought her first job
would have her running for her life—or crawling into
a stranger's bed....

ONE HOT NUMBER by Sandy Steen
May 2002
Accountant Samantha Collins may be good with numbers, but
she needs some work with men...until she meets sexy but
broke rancher Ryder Wells. Then she decides to make him a
deal—her brains for his bed. Sam's getting the better of the
deal, but hey, who's counting?

WHAT'S YOUR PLEASURE? by Julie Elizabeth Leto
June 2002
Mystery writer Devon Michaels is in a bind. Her publisher has
promised her a lucrative contract, *if* she makes the jump to
erotic thrillers. The problem: Devon can't write a love scene to
save her life. Luckily for her, Detective Jake Tanner is an
expert at "hands-on" training....

Don't miss this thrilling threesome!

HARLEQUIN®
Makes any time special ®

Visit us at www.eHarlequin.com

HTH

USA Today Bestselling Author

NAN RYAN

The Scandalous Miss Howard

The boy who left to fight in the
Confederate army twenty years ago
had been a fool. He had trusted the
girl who promised to wait for him.
He had trusted the friend who
betrayed him. Now he has come home
to Alabama to avenge the loss of what they
stole from him—his heart, his soul, his world.

Laurette Howard, too, lost her innocence with the
news that the boy she loved had died in the war, and
with the loveless marriage that followed. Then
Sutton Vane arrived in Mobile, releasing the sensual
woman that had been locked away. She surrendered
to a passion so scandalous, it could only be destiny.
But was it a passion calculated to destroy her...
or to deliver the sweet promise of a love that
refused to die?